Mizzly Fitch

Mizzly Fitch

Murray Andrew Pura

REGENT COLLEGE PUBLISHING
VANCOUVER, BRITISH COLUMBIA

Mizzly Fitch
Copyright ©1988 by Murray Pura

Reproduced 1998 by Regent College Publishing, an imprint of the Regent
College Bookstore, 5800 University Boulevard, Vancouver, B.C. V6T 2E4
email: bookstore@regent-college.edu
Website: www.regent-bookstore.com
Orders toll-free: 1-800-334-3279

The views expressed in this work are those of the author and do not necessarily
represent the official position of Regent College.

Printed in Canada

Cover image licensed through Corel Professional Photo CD © 1995.

Canadian Cataloguing-in-Publication-Data

Pura, Murray, 1954—
  Mizzly Fitch

I. Title.

PS8581.073M59   1987   C813'.54   C87-093572-0
PR9199.3.P87 M59   1988

ISBN 1-57383-127-1

Foreword

Mizzly Fitch is the lifestory of Cale Fitch, last surviving son from a family of Nova Scotia fisherman, and for 30 years a lighthouse keeper at Bushen's Reef, off the Nova Scotia coast. But to describe this deceptively short novel in that way would be like saying that Moby Dick is about a man chasing a whale, *The Odyssey* about a Greek adventurer who has a hard time getting home, or *The Rime of the Ancient Mariner* about a sailor who shot an albatross.

It is not frivolous to compare the book with those classics. *Mizzly Fitch* is a great novel—in its own way, it is a great poem—and it deserves to be read in the same company as those elemental stories about God, men and the sea.

Like all three of those works, it is about a struggle between man and God, with boats, sea and weather as the battlefield. We meet the theme early enough—on the second page.

> I used to get angry at God, you. The two of us, we'd already been at it
> right fierce for some years.... You need to understand that it was kind
> of cat and mouse game between God and me, I was always watching
> the sky, the sea, looking for a clue, anything that would give me the
> jump on him.

Like Melville's Ahab, Homer's Odysseus, and Coleridge's nameless Mariner, Mizzly feels that God—or the gods—is the enemy. Says the young Mizzly after two friends drown: "God done it, Dad, He's got the sea, He goes after the people. He's always done that, the Bible's full of it." But his parents, devout Christians, do not share his understanding. His father, with an apparent blindness that frustrates Cale, blames the bad on the sea ("that weren't nobody's fault, that's just the way life is") and thanks God for the occasional moments of beauty.

Cale... Look at this here, this blue and shining and these white birds just coasting on the wind... Look boy, it's all there for us, and there ain't no end to it. What kind of name do you give to the person who made it? What do you call him? Somebody that makes sea and light and wind, what kind of person is that?

One of Cale's brothers, lost at sea for days and given up for dead before he was picked up by a Gloucester boat, has no doubt that the sea is indeed the work of God: but after his night adrift on a wild sea firey with phosphorescence, he cannot rest easy with what he has seen of God, and he tells Cale, whom he still thinks is contemplating the ministry:

You know what I think? That it's all fire, every bit of it, the sea and the night, and all the land and the rock... it's all fire, everything out there is fire. I'm wondering, what keeps us from burning up? The only way I can see it, something holds the fire back. Some kind of god.... Now, I'm scared of the kind of strength that can keep it all in. What kind of thing is this, this god that holds back flame? That's why I'm telling you. You sure you want to get close to this? How do you know what it'll do to you?

Eventually, when all the family is dead except Cale's mother—and she, mad with grief, tries to kill him for being "the Devil's son" who brought it all about—he ends up on a lighthouse determined to save people whom God, through the sea, tries to kill: and through 30 years saves over a hundred from drowning. Every man saved from the sea, he believes, is a man saved from God's malice. Then *comes the day of Katrina E. Zwicker...the day of my dying*—another storm around the light, and the beginning of the end of Mizzly Fitch's long war with God.

On the surface, this is a regional story, full of language, the accents, the very smell and taste of the deeply-rooted fishing communities in Nova Scotia. Pura is originally from the Canadian prairies, and perhaps part of the book's eloquence and strength is—paradoxically—the impact of the sea on a prairie-shaped mind. Pura married a girl from a Nova Scotia fishing family, and the book was written out of years of living on the coast, in that culture, absorbing the stories of that centuries-old way of life.

Yet, like those other great tales of men, gods, and the sea with which I have compared *Mizzly Fitch* (each of which is also rooted in a particular maritime culture) this regional novel is deeply universal, and has a universal theme. For it is fundamentally a theodicy: a Job-like questioning of the mystery of evil in a world shot through with goodness. And like those other marine theodicies, its answers are not easy or comfortable.

Generations of pious language has tamed the great words of this novel's subtitle: *The Light, the Sea, the Storm.* Yet like all true literature, *Mizzly Fitch* releases the tamed mysteries, and restores our awe at being a person made both to ask hard questions of God—and wait for God's hard gracious answers.

— Loren Wilkinson

For a friend born and raised on the Atlantic, Linda, my wife

Acknowledgements

My thanks to the following people who helped my first novel see the light of day: Marian M. Wilson, my hard-working editor at Simon & Pierre; Dennis Mills, who spent so many hours helping me to hone the manuscript; Jennifer and Bob Doede, Steve and Paula Dunning, Richard and Goldie Levy, Linda Pura, and Loren Wilkinson, all of whom read early drafts of the book and made helpful suggestions; my family, especially my parents, Paul and Rose Pura, for their moral support spread over so many years; the staff and curators of The Fisheries Museum of the Atlantic in Lunenburg who have provided such a stimulating atmosphere for research; and finally, those people of Nova Scotia's South Shore who made a prairie boy their good friend and took me to the sea.

The
Light

The Light

No. I don't mind telling the story. I am Mizzly Fitch. And them two vessels, the *Heather B Sarty* and the *Katrina E Zwicker,* them and that lighthouse, why they's the spindle and wheel and foot that run my life out, I'm not likely to forget much about them, am I? The *Katrina E Zwicker,* she was in 1957, and she changed everything around with me. God knows why he'd cram your heart and soul into a couple of hours of a lifetime, but he done that. I got all of that day in my head yet.

I was keeper of the light at Bushen's Reef then, and that's about a half-mile's rowing out of Blue Rocks. Nobody called it Bushen's Reef, they called it Fitch's Rock, after me, because I was there a long time, thirty year or more. And the light was there, and they called that Fitch's Finger.

It was a dirty reef. It set right out there on the way into Lunenburg Harbour and yes, it caught a few. It was mostly under the water, you see, spreading out from the big rock they stuck the lighthouse on. A lot of times the men would be coming back from fishing two or three months at sea, and maybe they'd be tired, or they'd forget how far the rocks went out from the light. They put out a groaner to mark the edge of the reef, but you only seen it good when the weather was fine, and sometimes there wasn't nothing you could do to keep clear of the rocks, buoy or no. It was pitiful, you know, very sad, a man making it all the way back from the Banks and drowning there in sight of his own house.

I used to get some angry at God, you. The two of us, we'd already been at it right fierce for some years, and when a little boy got pitched overboard, the vessel he's on scraping the reef, that was it. I knowed the job would be up for keeper, the old boy Risser was retiring. The Department of Transport gave me the light, it's an uncle I had working for the government, and I moved right onto the Rock, took all I had with me.

Old Paul Risser now, he'd lived most of the time in Blue Rocks, staying on the reef only when the weather was bad. But for me it was, you know, a war. God was taking lives and I was right determined to take them back. I lived and ate and slept on that Rock, and I was only in town for supplies once or twice a month. Oh yes, it was some fight. I lit that light in 1928 when we was still using oil. I was eighteen then, and I stayed on till the *Katrina E Zwicker,* and I didn't lose no one, not in the hurricanes, or the snows, or the worst fog, no one. No. But a man, if he's fixed on fighting a god, has got to figure on a day coming when that god gets him in a corner and that's it. So that was the day of the *Katrina E Zwicker.*

It was the day of my dying. I'd rowed up to the dock in Blue Rocks, rowed over in my dory from the reef early in the morning. It was a fair day, a very fair day. The water was flat and green, like the back of a halibut, and it said nothing to me. You need to understand that it was a kind of cat and mouse game between God and me, I was always watching the sky, the sea, looking for a clue, anything that would give me the jump on him. But the sea said nothing to me that morning. Still, I didn't take my time in town. I had my list and I went down it pretty fast.

I never talked to the people in town much. They thought of me as a hermit or something, kind of odd, and most of them would nod at me, but not say anything. That was fine. I didn't want to talk. Oh, they was grateful for my job and the lives I'd saved, I knowed that, but they was afraid of me.

I was some big then, even at forty-seven, maybe six foot and five inches, lots of hard muscle, and somebody told me once that I had hands like spades. An old cut had pulled my right eye over towards the ear and nobody wanted to look at that eye. I come walking up from the dock once, the sky like charcoal, and Loren Richards says, "Look there, Fitch and the eye that God marked him with, dragging the sky down with him and the rain mizzling over his back." So they'd named me when I was still a young man, why I hadn't been on the Rock more than ten years when Richards spoke those words. It was Mister Fitch to my face, yes. But when I wasn't around it was Mizzly Fitch.

Now on that day of the *Zwicker*, there were two things happened in town just before I wheeled my barrow back down to the dock, and I saw them as signs that something was on the way. By the time I'd started back for the Rock, I'd put them together with some of the dreams I'd been having and with some of the things that had happened near the lighthouse, and it's then I says, "Fitch, perhaps this is it."

I'd been dreaming again and again about this graveyard, and wandering around in it, and finally falling asleep in it, sinking right below the grass, right into this black muck. I'd wake up and my heart was cracking my chest like a fist.

Then there'd been these dead birds all over the Rock. Never happened before, not to me. Sea duck and teal and gulls, maybe ten of them in a couple of weeks. That's when I start thinking that God is through playing with me, that he's going to finish me up, do the job he left undone on the *Heather B Sarty*. I guess I knowed he would be about it someday, that he was just toying with me down there at the light, making me think I really could beat him, beat back his killing and death.

It's these dreams and these dead birds gets me watching for God, gets me watching for how he's going to end my life. I pays careful attention to see if anyone ever lands at the Rock. No one ever does, just the inspector once a year. Still, I'm walking around and looking over my shoulder, knowing it's coming. Maybe I'll slip on a rock at night and go into the sea. Them stairs, them crazy narrow stairs winding up to the lantern, maybe I'll fall there, break my neck. Or a heart attack, I'm thinking. He could do that. Wonderful now, ain't it, the number of ways God has for killing a man?

All this I'm brewing up in my head when I gets in to Blue Rocks that day, and Lohnes at the general store, he says to me, "You think you'll have time to use up all this here, Mister Fitch?" I heard him all right. I looks at him right sharp and he sort of ducks his head down and sideways, pretending to fix up some bags or what. Then I'm outside loading my barrow and there's Harris Hardy leaning against his old truck, and he says, "Sorry to see you go, Mister Fitch." Just like that. Boys, it went right through me. Now, somebody would say, well, those two people didn't mean anything by it, they was just talking. But I knowed God was playing with me and that he meant me to hear what I heard, meant me to be afraid.

I pulled back to the Rock, working all this over, and I got surer and surer. This would be the day of God's coming. So I started looking at everything close, soaking it in, to have it sharp and clear, to have it with me.

It was some hot. It's maybe noon halfway to the Rock and the water sizzling and crackling around me like fire. It was late in August, a week to September, and cooking, cooking like a woodstove. Hurt to look at it. I was sweating so bad by the time I seen the light I began wondering if God was going to just broil me there, have done with me like some old lobster. I can joke about it some now, but it was a fierce heat, like the Devil were hauling his trawl through the cove.

The light. I come so's to fetch up in the little nook tucked just behind her, right where the rock is a flat shelf. There ain't any good place to land on the reef, and on a windy day you're dead if you try and get near, but on a calm day that little nook's as sweet a slip as you'll find. As I'm bringing her in, I'm looking back over my shoulder like I always do, watching that old light slide closer and closer. I liked that feeling, watching it move. When the dory hit the rock shelf I got out and pulled her up as far as I could, then I caught her up to her chain, huge old links I'd hammered right into the reef. There's a bit of a slope, slippery if there's waves, a patch of grass and weeds, some rock pools, and then the lighthouse, three stories.

I'd painted her fresh that June and she was gleaming like snow. Old Risser now, the keeper before me, he was pretty handy with the saw and hammer, he kept her up. Come out of his own pocket too. For me, it was my house, I was going to keep the light in good shape, no matter. She was old, maybe 1810, wood, clinging to that reef rock like she'd growed up out of it. I lived on the bottom floor, stored some gear and a bit of oil on the second. The third floor was empty, and then there was the lantern. It was a simple life.

Sometimes I felt like a sort of Greek Spartan, you know, holding the enemy back at some narrow gap. Then a monk, I tell you, yes, I used to think I was a monk in one of these high towers, keeping a fire lit against the barbarians and the dark. Oh no, I saw no difference between the Devil and God. They was both alike, them two. The one there killing with guns and bombs, the other with nature.

I stayed on the Rock during the war. I was only twenty-nine when Hitler invaded Poland, but I had my own war, a bigger war to fight, didn't I? I believe if one of them U-boats had come up there by the Rock, busting up from a storm, I would of saved her if I could, yes, I would of done it, because my war was different, and if God was trying to kill anyone it wouldn't of mattered to me what country they come from, I would of done everything to bring them alive from the sea. I was set right hard, yes, set right hard against him.

The boats was still coming in and out of Lunenburg during the war, the fish, to bring the fish in, that was right important. And I was there with my light. Saved a couple of the boats too. The first was in '41 or '42, in December. The *Stacey O'Connell,* a Yankee out of Portsmouth.

She come on out of this blow of snow and ice, oh, blowing like a bull, making the whole lighthouse shake, and she come in, but she didn't know the harbour well, she caught the reef. She was hulled pretty quick, and I seen they couldn't get her off, the waves was thrashing all around them, full of white. I didn't have no radio to call for help out of Lunenburg. If those men was going to make it, it was me going to have to get them off. I knowed my way about the reef in my boat, so I tied a strong hemp to that chain on the rock. What you had there was a long rope, and I paid it out as I paddled down to them.

It was a disgusting night, full of cold, and the wind just screaming, and them waves! Why, look, them waves was six, seven feet, and the come out of the dark like mountains. God batted me around like some wood chip, but we rode her down, you. Got to the boat and she was broke in half, her men all on the stern piece, and I held right in there, gripping that rope tight, till they'd all dropped into the dory, all five of them.

"Haul," I says. "Haul back on the rope."

They wasn't much for hauling then, half froze and wet and scared, and the dory didn't move. I was sure we was going to be swamped, some big wave breaking right into us.

"Haul!" I yells. "Haul or we're under!"

"No use," shouts one of them. "We're stiff as ice. We're going nowheres. Guess this is our night."

"It ain't nobody's night," I hollers right back to him. "We're two hundred yards from the lighthouse. Now, you haul on the rope and you'll sweat some and you'll be all right. Go on!"

So they started hauling back, and me using the oars, and the waves start breaking over us, filling the boat, and it's getting heavier and heavier, harder and harder to haul. But them Yankees kept at it, they had some hope again, and their blood was going.

That was two hundred miles more like. I hardly seen anything like it for being out in a small boat and I was some years on the Banks too, before I come to the Rock. The water was all white, white, like that old Wentzel's beard, flying every which way. And noise! It's like we weren't even in the world no more, weren't even on the earth.

But we come out of it. Got them all in. Hauled her right up to the flat of rock, and the waves, they just throwed us onto the reef. We got to the house and I got some coffee and rum into them. The next day I seen the dory had a hole in it, I guess it come when we was pitching onto the reef at the end. Some would say it was luck, but no, it was a fight, a good fight, you.

The other, the *Christina Covey*, there was another that never knowed the harbour, why, she come in full throttle, full throttle into the Rock now, right into the hill back of the light. There weren't no storm a'tall, and it just come night, the water as sweet as cream. She figured she could come down behind the light, and I seen her doing it, and I started blowing the foghorn, but it made no difference to her. Right into the steep of the Rock, broke all to pieces. If there'd of been a wind blowing, I don't believe I could of got them out. But I clamped a lantern onto the bow of the dory and I come down to them in good time, fished them all out, there were, I think, four. Some shook up. But the boat, a beautiful new boat, there was a shame, not even enought left for the wrackers.

I saved a few, but I couldn't be everywhere and God could, and I heard all the time them years about boats going down, all hands, out by Sable, or on the Banks, or worse yet, maybe just up the coast a few mile. That was hard, real hard to take. Lost a number of boys out of Blue Rocks once, me sitting in the lantern, the light shining for nothing, them dying a couple of miles off, just by Pearl. God knowed that would hurt. He knowed it would eat at me, him hauling in all these boys I couldn't touch. I got out on the lantern deck one night, and I leaned into that rail, and I yelled, I want to tell you, yelled right at him, called him a coward, told him to set me down wherever he did his work and we'd see who had the better of it. But all that hollering, as you might of guessed, it come to nothing. He's just laughing the harder, I thought. So I shut up, and I just backed and waited for his next move.

It weren't always boats he'd come at me with. No. I'd never planned to stay a bachelor, and after eight years on the Rock, when I was about twenty-six, I had my eye out. I used to come into Blue Rocks or Lunenburg for the dances, started coming in regular. But God, he done his work. Already by then they seen me as a queer fish, wouldn't have nothing to do with me. I was already Mizzly Fitch to them, and it was already Fitch's Rock, and they painted me in some colours. Had the girls all scared to come near me. It was terrible. I'd cross the floor to ask this girl to dance with me and she was just disgusted I'd asked, or she'd go white, and that happens to you too many times, you ain't about to go back at it, are you? Then, of course, I got in a fight. You might of knowed some of the boys wanted to have a go at me and see if they could come out on top. I broke a few heads and you can imagine how that went over. In the end, it was just me and the Rock and my living. God had set it out just right.

There was one girl now, she was some nice, hair like a run of sun and water, she tried to get to know me. I ain't figured out to this day whether she was one of them that's got to rebel with something, and I was handy, or whether she really did like me. She'd talk to me in town, sometimes be at the dock when I come in, this years after I quit going to the dances. I don't say it was easy for her. I wasn't much of a talker anymore, and I seen her get her share of looks from people, they was disgusted with her, that she would come on to me. Something might of been made out of it too. Said she'd never knowed a fellow like me, that she'd be back for me after she'd tried a bit of city life. God knows why she wanted it. She packed up and left for Halifax just before the war. That was it. I found out what come of her though. Married a soldier and went back to Saskatchewan with him when the war was over. I don't know what he done for a living. Farming, I guess. That was my one big romance. That's something, ain't it? That's something how God cut me right off there on the reef. No women, no friends, nothing. It was a dirty war. Yes, a real dirty war.

Let me tell you, I got some of my own back though. In all them years it was fifteen or twenty boats come onto the reef, and I pulled almost a hundred men out of her. A hundred men! How many's can say they done that with their work, saved a hundred lives? If I'd of been a fireman they would of decorated me, wouldn't they, made a real hero out of me.

Oh, there were some sweet things done. Willard Joudrey now, weren't he something? Cared nothing for God or religion. You seen him there, big face as red as a kipper, always shifting his weight, eyes up and about, no peace to him. Salt banker captain, then went and opened his own tavern in Bridgewater. Used to drop down and sail a boat he had, had a boat and a small house in Blue Rocks, kept them both up long after he was living there in Upper La Have.

He was full of spit. Was drunk once and beat up a clergyman, yes, he done that, an Anglican, don't know why, the Devil got in him when he was drinking. Made it a point, I remember, to dump his dories over the rail on Sundays back in the days he skippered a vessel. Some men kicked up a fuss, but some went over and didn't they get fish. So them others would be going at it Sundays too before long, can you imagine? Why look, it just weren't done then, didn't matter you was religious or no. But Joudrey done it. He was a real high liner. Didn't care. And his men made money, though they wasn't going to boast about setting out their trawls on a Sunday. Yes, they made their money, so they'd head out with him again and go at it.

Some hell-raiser that Joudrey was. You ought to seen Lunenburg liven up when he come in from the summer fishing. Down the streets in his pea jacket, hollering and throwing bottles, and sometimes money too, that's so. Money was never too much to him. It was taking risks he liked, doing something nobody would do. Like that fishing on Sundays. Do you suppose the boys would of stayed on with him if they didn't get fish or somebody had of drowned some Sunday afternoon? Oh no, they would of said it was bad luck coming on Joudrey because he was fishing on the Lord's Day, and they would of left him pretty quick once they'd got back into Lunenburg. Nobody would of gone out with him then. That would of finished him. But look you, it never happened. He done marvellous. That way with everything he set about doing. Until the morning off of the Rock.

You'd figure God would want that Joudrey down anytime he could get him, such a blasphemous man, with no use for the church or anything of God's. I was always wondering when he'd come for Joudrey, and he come that day, quick and sharp. That was in 1947, and Joudrey's out in a big wind in a little sailing dinghy, a crazy man, scooting in and around Rose Point and West Ironbound, and doesn't it come a big blow and split his mast like a twig, I guess. Just broke it in two. How he got in for Blue Rocks, I don't know. I seen him coming across the Bay, full of water and a stump for the mast. He lost the sail and spar, couldn't fish them out, they was just gone in that sea. So here he's rowing, rowing against that wind, and I tell you, it would tear the coat off your back.

He tried to clear the reef on the south side so's he could tuck right into Blue Rocks. But he had no strength left. Couldn't keep her into the waves and she broached. It took maybe a minute for a big wave to hit her and she was gone, went right under, and Joudrey with hardly enough in him to stay up, let alone keep off of the rocks. That was God's way. To sweep him into the rocks and crack him open. But I was already coming down on him before his boat went, had a sail up and was coming down on him, the wind being a sou'easter. A cruel wind too, and it's killed a lot of men, but that day it brings me right up to Joudrey as neat as you'd want. I gets him in half drowned, and his pea jacket sopping, and his fingers like ice, but alive. He lies there in the bottom of the dory and I throws some canvas over him, and he's shivering, and looking at me, and he says, "Thank God, it's over."

"No, old man," I says, "it sure ain't over. This is just it now."

I had to row back into that sou'easter with Joudrey there, three hundred pounds and soaking. Couldn't use no sail now. So I sets to paddling and look, it comes up a bigger blow than before. I digs in and pulls and it seems like nothing's happening, the boat don't hardly seem to move. I'd had that kind of rowing before, heading back to the vessel with five tubs of trawl, and you and your partner half dead from hauling all afternoon. It was work, and you felt like you was getting nowhere. I digs in harder, the water boiling all around me like a pot, and I says, "Fitch, this is your fight now. Don't lose her." And I pulled, and I kept her nose into the waves, and it must of been two hours to go that six hundred feet, I'm telling you. When I got her in behind the lighthouse my hands was all over blood, all these blood blisters had been coming up and breaking, but I hadn't felt it because my hands were pretty near frozen.

That was some battle, but I won it, and it felt so good to get a soul back from God, especially a soul like Joudrey, somebody I knowed God hated and wanted so bad he'd bring a whole wind around to do his work. That was a good day. Joudrey now, he weren't one to forget that, take it for granted like some others. Every year he was alive he was sending me food and liquor and a lot of things I'd never of bought, could never of afforded. Every year he had them brought over to the Rock, I believe, yes, the same day every year, the day I'd pulled him from the sea.

Getting Joudrey back, now that was satisfying, but it weren't the most satisfying. There was a lobster man named Arthur Crouse, and when his boat hit the reef, well, that was better, getting him out, that was a lot better. He'd taken his four kids out with him that day, all little girls, some sweet, you, and none of them over seven. I seen them once dressed up for church. They was all the size of sandpipers and was about as restless. Brown as nuts them, and careful eyes, and faces fine, some fine carving there.

That was something. Them girls, they wasn't afraid of me. I was sitting at the dock, just looking out at the water, and it was lovely warm, and they come by, shy at first, then going at her. Asking was I Mizzly Fitch the lightkeeper, and would I take them out up to the reef sometime to see the lighthouse, and when did I turn the light on and off, and all this here. They made me laugh. Their father come to get them, but Arthur, he was all right, smiling at me, giving me a nod as he got them into the car. Quiet he was, and small, but taut, and tough as a cable. Hair was like a tangle of dulse, and he always wore a pair of black-framed glasses, strong things, his eyes behind them strong and dark too, like stones in the water.

I'm not faulting Arthur for what happened. It was early spring and the sea was smooth and green as the lawn of some country club. He'd set out his traps a week before and he'd promised the girls to take them out sometime when he hauled them up. I seen him heading out from Blue Rocks and he blew his horn as he went by. I gave him a blast back.

What God had in for Arthur, I don't know. He was a deacon in the Baptist church and a good father, a good working man. But God, he'll go for his own like as not. I never understood that. It seemed savage to me, like God was just some shark tearing at anything near him. Oh, he come after Arthur in an awful hurry.

A religious person might of tried to soften it all, but there weren't no softening it. The squall only hit that part of the Bay Arthur was at, and when he come running in for Blue Rocks, it followed him like it were tied right into him. He almost got by the reef, but his prop scraped some rock and that was it gone. Once I seen him lose way, I was in my oils and down to the dory.

It was hammering rain, and there was a big swell, but I got out and around the edge of the Rock. It was a fearful thing. That squall hauled Arthur right over the reef, the whole length of it pretty near, and it crushed him up against the bottom of the cliff, just below the lighthouse. The bottom was tore out of that boat, and the only reason she was still up, she was wedged in there between a couple of big rocks sticking out of the water. I come up, I don't know when I ever rowed like that again. The sea took me into a few good rocks and they took a strip out of my boat. But I got right under Arthur's bow and that was a bit of shelter, I could get in close and get them off.

Those girls weren't even whimpering. They was wet and scared, I could see that, but there weren't no crying. Arthur dropped each of them down into the boat, it was all I could do to keep the dory in close. A couple of them got banged up, the youngest sprained her ankle kind of bad, but there still weren't no hollering, some tears and that's it. Arthur timed his jump bad, went down between the rocks and the dory, and I feared for him. But he come up and hauled himself into the boat, some blood on his face, but all right, holding his glasses in his hand.

"Thank you, Fitch," he shouts.

"We're not out of it yet, Arthur," I yells. "Them rocks almost took me apart on the way in. You might want to wait and thank me later, maybe."

"No," he shouts. "No, this is fine now."

Doesn't he get in amongst them girls and have a prayer with them. And as I'm pulling out into the wind, he's got them singing, why, it's like they was sitting in the front pew of their church, warm and dry. I can see it yet. The boat pitching and yawing, the wind blowing spray hard into my face, me pulling at the oars, pulling for all I'm worth, and them girls sitting in a bunch around their father, sitting and singing that hymn. That was some ride. Them singing and the wind howling and me looking straight at them the whole time. I got to feeling I was a Pentecostal or something.

And then, what do you think? The wind drops, and we still got a good swell, but it ain't hard now, ain't difficult a'tall. Why look, by the time we're bringing the dory in to the Rock the sun's blazing and the sea's full of light. God put a good one over and I had to laugh.

They stayed on for a bit, drying off and putting themselves together. We got some ice on Rose's ankle, got Arthur's face cleaned up and some sticking plaster on his forehead where the rocks had sliced him. Of course, the girls had to see it all, so I carried Rose up them stairs to the lantern and the others trooped along behind. It's a funny thing. Rose was the youngest, but she was their leader, and Mary had two years on her. Was Rose decided who went where when, it seemed like, and when Sarah starts asking about something to eat, it's Rose tells her not to be impolite, but to wait until I offers. It's the way Rose was with her sisters, and they took it.

You might of knowed they'd love the light. I tried to explain everything to them, the two lamps with their silver reflectors, the springs that move the lamps in a circle, the crank you use to wind the springs up, yes, they all had to give that a turn. Then there was the pan of mercury that keeps the lamps steady when the lighthouse is shaking in the wind, and that's a wonder to them. I finish showing them how the oil feeds into the lamps and they decide they want to wait until night to see how the lamps look when they're lit. Arthur didn't mind staying, I could see that, but he was worried about his wife, that somebody might of seen the boat go down but not seen me take them off. I tell him I can call up Margaret Bushen on the radio they just put in, it's her job to pass any messages on and she can let Paula know they're all right. Arthur was still a bit fidgety, but he seen the girls wanted to stay and he wanted to to that for them. So I got ahold of Margaret Bushen, said all the Crouses was fine, that I'd bring them in to Blue Rocks in the morning.

Arthur and me fried up some fish and chips for the bunch of us.

When it come to lighting the lamps, that was always kind of a ritual with me, and they respected that, following me up real quiet, Rose right snug in my arms, her eyes dark and taking it all in. I had my charts, always lit up an hour before sunset, unless there was storm or fog. I remember it was sharp clear that night. A couple of the boys going into Lunenburg winked back and this got the girls going.

"We're taking care of all them fishermen, ain't we, Mister Fitch?" asks Becky.

"That's right," I says. "This light sees them in safe."

"What does the light look like from out there?" asks Rose.

"Oh, it's like gold," I tells her, "sparkles like gold."

"Is it brighter than the lights of the houses in Blue Rocks?" asks Mary.

"I guess it is," I says. "Were you out on a boat now, you could pick out our light just like that. A lot brighter than the lights in Blue Rocks."

Then I remember Rose asking, "Is our boat still down there now?"

You could look down and just see part of her deck and hull. "Yes," I says, "but I believe she'll be gone by morning."

"She was a good boat," says Rose. "She was a good boat, weren't she, Dad?"

"She were fine," says Arthur.

We come down soon after that, but Arthur stayed up there a bit. It ain't easy for a man to have a boat go out from under him, never mind the danger of it. He'd been fetching up lobster from that boat for ten year. Maybe it ain't the same as the old days when you had a sailing vessel under your feet, living and breathing and talking to you, but a man's working boat is, you know, a partner like. You're losing a life when she goes. So Arthur stayed up for a time, and I didn't say nothing, and the girls didn't ask.

I had a bunch of army cots and I shoved them together and got the girls under some point blankets. There was a couple of oil lamps lit and I sticks a fat candle near the cots.

"Mister Fitch," says Rose, "it ain't right you put us to bed without a story."

"Well, what'll it be then?" I asks, and I sits down there on a chair facing the four of them.

"Ghost stories," goes Rose.

"All right," I says. "Does you know the story of the *Young Teazer*?"

"Oh, we knows that one too well," says Mary. "You must give us something new."

"Oh, I see," I says.

But a story come to me and I starts telling it, stooped over with my hands on my knees. I had the past keepers of the light come up from the grave to judge me, to judge my work at the light. But all the time I'm telling them this here, putting blood on the walls and drowned men sagging in the chairs, crawling about at the back of my mind is the night I seen a body below the lighthouse, a body in old clothing, a body impaled on a broken spar, spitting seawater and vomit, eyes gouged out by the gulls and the crabs. God, I run down and the man was still alive, trying to speak to me, but as soon as I lifted his head it turned to grubs and weed in my hand. The first lightkeeper had thrown himself from the lantern deck, speared his body on the wreckage of a frigate that had gone down the day before. By the time I'd finished the story to the girls, I was feeling the dark of the night myself.

"I think we'd all like to go to sleep now," Rose whispers, "but Dad usually tells us a Bible story so's we can sleep better. Last night he told us about Jonah. Jonah was angry at God, Mister Fitch. He run from God. But a whale ate him. He had to live in the whale's stomach. It was black and full of rotten fish, just terrible. The whale spat him out onto a beach when Jonah told God he was sorry.''

"All right," I says. "But I have a better story than that."

And I told them about Job, how God took all his family and left him to die, how he cursed God, how in the end God said Job had been right in saying what he said. Then I blew out their candle.

"Good night," I says, and I steps over to sit by the stove. They whispers a bit and then it's all quiet in there and I'm just sitting and, you know, listening to nothing, and that wood snaps and snaps.

Arthur had been standing at the bottom of the stairs, I knowed that. He come over and he pulls up a chair and he's looking down at his hands. His body was like a length of hemp, but his hands, they was small, and almost smooth, as if he were in some office job and not a lobster man. He's still looking down and he says, "You ought to have a family. It ain't right, a man out here alone."

"No," I says, "it's all right."

"Nothing but wind and ocean," he keeps on, "and nobody you can talk with. It ain't decent."

"No," I tells him, "I never looks on it that way. It's a proper place to be. It's good work. I don't want anything else."

He looks up at me then. "You don't want nothing more?"

"No," I says. "I can't see it changing for me."

Arthur puts his head down again and I think that might of been it, but it were all of a sudden, I had it in me to talk.

The Sea

The Sea

It were all right with God and me at the beginning. We hit it off fine then. Of course, there was nothing to come along to test the strength of the friendship, you know, nothing to come at it and see what it was worth. That come later. I don't say God was all in the wrong. But I guess he could of done things differently.

I was born on East Tarragon, just near Big Tancook. I think it always was, most of the people on Tarragon was religious, most of the families took it right serious. I suppose that was more generally the case all around, where now you don't see so much of it. If some of them had come through what I did, they'd of changed their way of looking at things.

There weren't no church on that island, there weren't enough people for that. Once a month maybe a preacher would come in, then all the families would get together in one of the homes. I'm not saying they was bad times. Henry Manthorne, Hank, he used to be the preacher for years. I don't know where he was all the rest of the time, but it was twelve or fifteen years he come into Tarragon. He was all right. Went over with everybody because he'd eat what you put in front of him and he liked to go out in the boats.

He used to get to the island in his own little dinghy, a sailing dinghy. Didn't matter what the weather was like. I don't believe he hardly missed a visit. I remember there was a winter storm once and it smashed in a couple of the boats. There was no stopping that wind, it would come right in off the sea and nothing to break it. We was all up in our houses burning wood, playing checkers, and it was Saturday afternoon. Charlie Zinck, he used to keep the light there and do some fishing too, Charlie come banging on our door, because Dad, he was like a kind of head deacon, he used to preach all the other Sundays when there weren't no minister. Charlie's banging at our door and Mom lets him in and he was soaking, had no oils on a'tall, no sou'wester, nothing. He'd come running right from the lighthouse and he come down just in his shoes and pants and shirt. Water all over Mom's floor and Charlie almost shouting at her.

"Missus Fitch! It's Hank's boat coming in! I believe he just lost his sail!"

I remember Dad walking in at that and he says to me, "Cale, get your brothers and down to the landing. Mother, we'll bring Hank up."

So I gets my four brothers and they're off and into their oils and me, I'm the youngest, I'm trailing them down to the landing. Dad was already there and he says, "No, he won't make it in here, maybe down the lee shore some," and he was right, Hank wasn't about to make it in to the landing in that wind and without a sail. He sort of blows out of sight around the north side of the island, the lee side. "Come on," says Dad, "maybe he'll fetch up yet, the crazy fool," but I seen Dad smiling, he thought a lot of the man, coming out in such weather.

We ran over to the north shore and we couldn't see him, and then Dad was afraid he'd gone down. We was all beginning to feel terrible when Hank comes up and says, "Afternoon, Mister Fitch. Wicked to the world, ain't it?" Oh, that was something. He'd fetched up further down and had started over to the houses when he seen us. And he was laughing. Dad said later he was probably laughing the whole time he was in the boat too, like some big kid out in the waves and not knowing enough to be scared.

We got him down to the house and by then most of the men were there, and Hank says, "I'll have the men in the parlour right away, I got some things I want to say before the families get together," and in they troops. You had to be eighteen for them men's meetings and I was only twelve at the time. That used to annoy me, yes. I'd already been out my first season on the Banks and here I was left with the children and the women. I never got into one of Hank's meetings for the men. All I can say about them is you heard a lot of laughter coming through the door.

When Hank would come in, usually by the Saturday night, we'd have ourselves a bit of preaching and a hymn sing till ten or eleven o'clock. Then there'd be a proper service the next day in somebody's home and the men would be in their suits of blue serge. How Hank preached, he'd straddle a kitchen chair front to back and just start in. You talk about your money's worth. Hank would go on for two hours, like as not, and no one wanting him to stop neither, except your backside would get sore. He could put a sermon together. It weren't like the kind where you feel you're in some big city church. He talked like a man would talk to you out in the boats and you're hauling trawl. Stories! Why, he was full of them and I only heard him repeat a couple in all the years he come in.

He'd be setting there, big hands over the back of the chair, and your eyes was always on his face. A bunch of curly black hair Mom was always saying was too long, a face round as a pan, and big eyes that made me think of a couple of brass door knobs. His teeth were bad and his body was heavy, so we seen a good bear in him, we boys.

I never seen Jesus as this here blonde woman walking white lambs through the sky, never. It used to be Jesus was as rugged and natural to me as any man in the fishing fleet. In them days, I'd talk to Jesus, you know, sitting out watching the sun come up, or out and walking in the woods, it were all the same, Jesus was real. That's what Hank could do, he brought it all down into your hands like. It wasn't none of it far away.

So he'd finish up a Sunday morning and there'd be some feast. The women would of baked some meat and some pies and all of that. Then come the real good time, just Hank and the children. I guess I didn't mind being twelve then. He'd take us out walking, didn't matter what the weather was, and out would come more stories. I tell you, he had us believing Jesus and the disciples lived in a cove on the west side of the island, and that Peter had a boat there they used to get around Mahone Bay and all down the South Shore. Halifax, that was Jerusalem. Capernaum, that was Tarragon. Mahone Bay was the Sea of Galilee, and all this here. Imagine Jesus in a sou'wester and oils, preaching and handing out cod to feed the people from Lunenburg and Blue Rocks, and us not even finding it ridiculous. He could do it, Hank could do it.

We'd be back for a big supper, and then Hank getting us around the woodstove to sing hymns, and then another sermon, only this one would be more careful and slow, but he could still make us listen. All them fishermen, Dad, and Bill and Ernie Zinck, and Robert and Angus Young, the bunch of them, sitting as if they was listening to hear the call to get up their tubs and over the rail for the fish. Yes, that was something.

I don't say all the preachers was like Hank. I knowed one in Lunenburg thought he was the High King of Ireland. There was a lot like that, all their schooling and big cloaks and whiskers, but then there was Hank too.

I believe Dad would of been up with the best of them, but he couldn't leave the sea. When he was home for the winter, I'd always see him setting in his chair and reading his father's Bible in the light of the oil lamp. Isaac Fitch had been lost at sea before I was born, but his sea chest come home with the vessel and Dad was the oldest of the boys, so he got the Bible. Even out on the Banks it was the same, Dad reading the Bible with a bit of candle, and that after all the fishing and the dressing down, all of them cold hours out on the sea. God was something stitched right into Dad's heart and soul. You couldn't have one without the other.

Dad was, I would say, a strong man, a very strong man, and just over six foot, but do you think he ever put the fear of God in me? "Look, boy," he'd say when I got myself in trouble, "I want to come to an understanding with you." So he'd walk me down to the old shed where we kept the fishing gear, our fish store, and have us mucking about with the cod and the salt and the nets, and he'd say, "Boy, these take me out to God and everything that's good," and after an hour or two he'd walk me back up to the house and that would be it. He'd get me stitching nets or checking the salt cod, and it always put me in the mind of what it was I wanted to be, which was a man, and a fisherman, and that always made me want to act more grown up. So Dad knowed what he was doing and he never laid a hand on me, not on any of us.

He had a temper. I hardly seen it come on but for a few times on the Banks. Once it was one of the men out of Riverport was cussing up a storm and Dad got fed up with it, went over to him and told him to shut his mouth and his fists were bunched by his sides. The man, he stops cussing right quick, I can tell you. Another time it was a man doing a bit of handlining over the side of the vessel on a Sunday and Dad cut the line with a knife right when the man's hauling her up taut with a big fish. That fellow, he come looking for blood, but Dad says to him, "You want to fight, we'll fight her good after the Sabbath. But I'll put up with no Jonah on this boat." The man could see Dad meant business and he did nothing more about it.

The only time I ever saw Dad use his fists was a time in Lunenburg when he seen a man beating his wife in public, and he laid that man right out. I think if Dad hadn't been a religious man, if he'd been the kind of man who went for a drink, it could of been very hard for us. But our life was good there on Tarragon. Oh, good, but he was laying in wait, God was playing out our line, making us feel fine, and there he's waiting for the right day, the right hour to haul up.

It was my Uncle Tremaine he come after first. We were back into Lunenburg after the summer fishing. I'd gone out for the first time the year before, when I was eleven, and now I was twelve and just finishing my second trip as a header. It was 1922. We was coming up from the vessel when the captain of Uncle Tremaine's boat come over to Dad and told him. Uncle Tremaine hadn't been close to any of us, but it was the first time anybody had been lost in our family since Dad's father drowned. I went to bed thinking of Uncle Tremaine sitting there in a black sou'wester and oils.

He had a face like a fish does, long and wide-eyed and blank. He'd come over to Tarragon to visit and just sit in a corner of the house, his hands flat in his lap, palms up, and he'd watch the rest of us carrying on. He'd work at a piece of food the way a cod works its mouth when it's still alive and lying in the bottom of the boat. I can't even remember his voice. One of the men told Dad it was like working with a phantom to sit in a dory with him and haul trawl.

I dreamed about him drowning almost every night for two weeks.

He'd be sinking down through the water, eyes wide open and not even blinking, his mouth working, black oils on and his hands over his head, fingers trailing through the water. One night he starts to swim about like a fish, arms close to his sides, moving slowly through the water in his black oils, bubbles sliding out of the black hole of his mouth. There's a hook full of bait comes dangling over his head and he swims up to it and closes his mouth over it. They haul back on the hook and it rips through his throat and they take him up, but there's no blood. Who brings him in but a big old man, and don't he take a long blade and set to dressing Uncle Tremaine as neat as you'd want, splitting him throat to crotch with one stroke, slashing off his head, yanking out his guts. I woke up screaming, and then I started vomiting. It was Mom come to me, and she held onto me till I stopped yelling and heaving, and it didn't matter to her it was all over her housecoat. She were big, almost as big as Dad, and heavier, and she held me so's I couldn't move, and after a while I quieted down and she cleaned me up.

"All right," says Mom. "Your uncle's dead and gone now. He ain't no fish and nobody's going to hook him. His body's gone deep and his soul's gone to God. Everything is fine now."

But it weren't fine. Even after my nightmares ended, I kept thinking about Uncle Tremaine getting hooked and hauled up into that old man's boat. One day that winter, it must of been right after my thirteenth birthday in January, I was reading some old book I found under a bunch of boxes in the basement. It was about all the gods of Rome and Greece, and there was the old man in the boat. They named him Jupiter or Zeus, but it was the same hair and body and all of it. So I read about this god and it frightened me because he was cruel. I got to wondering if Hank's God and Dad's God were the same as this Zeus god.

One night I come to Dad sitting by his oil lamp with Grandad Isaac's Bible and I asks, "Dad, who killed Uncle Tremaine?"

"Nobody killed your uncle," he tells me. "The sea took him."

"No, Dad," I says. "I had a dream about God handlining, and he hauled up Uncle Tremaine and dressed him neat and quick. I believe it was God took Uncle Tremaine."

"Look, boy," my Dad says, getting right serious, "here's what it is. Your uncle was out in the dory and a breeze come up, and a big wave flipped the dory over, and both your uncle and another man was drowned. Now, that were an accident, pure and simple. God took your uncle home to heaven all right, but he didn't kill him. The sea did that. You see what I'm saying?''

I turned this over for a week or two and then I come to Dad again where he's reading grandad's Bible next to the oil lamp.

"Dad," I asks, "ain't God greater than the sea?"

"Of course," he says, not even looking up. "God made the sea."

"You mean the things God makes ain't greater than him?"

"No."

"But if you makes a boat, ain't the boat greater than the man who makes it? It's bigger and stronger and it can sail all over the world."

"No, not by itself it can't," Dad says, his eyes on me. "It needs a man to steer it and put its sails right. It's the man controls the boat. That makes the man greater, you see."

"If that's so," I tells him, "God is the one who controls the sea and tells it what to do, and it was God who killed Uncle Tremaine."

Dad put his Bible aside right quick at that, and he leaned over close to me. "Boy," he says, "are you pulling my leg?"

"No, Dad," I answers him. "That's the way I see's it."

Weren't Dad upset at me thinking that. Not angry upset, but hurt, you know, that one of his sons would think that way about God. What happened was, the next time Hank come over, he gets me alone out in the woods on the east end of the island, and he sits down with me on a big rock.

"Cale," Hank says to me, "you been having bad dreams about your uncle that drowned."

"Yes," I says, "I had some, but I don't anymore."

"But you think about it a lot, don't you?"

"Yes."

"You want to tell me what the dreams were like?"

So I tells Hank about the dreams and the book and the talks with Dad, how the sea is controlled by God, the one who made it.

"Cale," he says, "what if I were to tell you that it was the Devil in the boat hauling up and splitting your uncle?"

"Do you mean the Devil killed my uncle?"

"Maybe."

"Then the Devil must be greater than God."

"What do you mean?"

"The Devil must of got control of the sea, he must of got it away from God. How else could he drown Uncle Tremaine if God's the one that runs the world and runs the sea?"

"All right, all right. Suppose the Devil sent you the dream to confuse you?"

"Oh. I don't know."

"He could do that, couldn't he?"

"I suppose he could."

"After all, God doesn't send dreams to frighten people."

"Not even when they've been bad?"

"No, I don't think so. God doesn't work that way."

"But somebody drowned Uncle Tremaine, somebody that controls the sea."

"Look now, Cale," says Hank and he puts his arm around me. "It was a bad wind and it flipped your uncle's boat and it wasn't anybody's fault. It's just the way the world is."

"So God isn't in control of the world or the sea? There's nothing God could of done about Uncle Tremaine drowning?"

"It's not that God couldn't do anything. It's just that he decided not to. He decided to take him home."

"So God did kill him."

"God took him."

"What's the difference?"

"There's lots of difference. Because God took him to heaven and God knows when the time is right for that."

"Why couldn't he take him when he was sleeping? Why'd God have to choke him and drown him?"

"I don't know, Cale," says Hank, "but I know God ain't cruel. I know he don't go hunting for men the way men go hunting for fish."

I guess I got to be a thorn in everyone's side. Mom had a book of Bible stories she used to read out loud to us every night before bed, to me and the twins Matthew and Aaron anyway, who were just seventeen, and I got to asking her questions about all of them stories too, stories I'd heard since I was knee-high. Why did God let the Devil kill all of Job's children just for a bet? Why did God throw Jonah into a whale instead of just talking to him the way Dad did with me when I wasn't acting right? Why was God so rough with

Moses, not letting him see the Promised Land because of one mistake? Why did God always want all those animals cut up and burned for him? Why was he always telling Joshua to wreck towns and kill people? Why did he let Jesus get murdered? Why did everything God put his hand to wind up with somebody dying? It got so the Bible story time petered out, and Mom started getting right cross with me. It was Dad took my side when she'd get on me.

"I don't know what we're raising," she'd say.

"Never mind," Dad would tell her. "He's got a mind of his own and that's more than I can say for a lot of men three times his age, always going this way and that like a lot of wood smoke in a breeze."

"Oh, a mind of his own he's got, but it ain't a mind for God and it ain't a mind for religion. You watch out where he goes," she'd say.

"Let him be. The Lord can turn a Saul, he can turn a Cale. Thank God the boy's got some spirit to him. Look at the other boys his age. There's nothing to them a'tall."

"Well, you sound as if you're proud of the kind of questions he's asking."

"I'm proud that he's got the guts to ask them. Who's got a boy like Cale on this island, you tell me, who's got a boy the whole South Shore as sharp as him? Let him be."

Mom would back down when Dad was home, but if she got me alone and her mind was into it, she'd light right into me. One day she was going on about how good God was and how wise God was and how loving God was and how bad I was not to treat God as well or better than I did my earthly father, and all this here. I takes a glass and throws it across the room and it breaks all over the wall and the floor. I shouts at her, "The hell with God! He's a bloodthirsty old bugger. I wish Dad were God. He ought to be. He's a lot more human."

She come at me then, and I was getting big at thirteen, but she got ahold of me and hit me across the face with her fist, then she just whaled into me, knocked me down and dragged me out of the house and swore she wouldn't let me in the door again. I ran out to the woods and Dad come later and found me there. "Let's go down to the store," he says, and so we went down and lit the lanterns. He got me sanding down our gaffs, and he's sitting there with these hooks over his knees, and he says to me, "Cale, I think we'll do some winter fishing this year, just the two of us, up and around the

Bay here. We'll do some handlining and some trawling both. I want you ready when we heads out with the fleet in June for the summer trip. I have it in me to ask Captain Himmelman to sign you on as a doryman. I want you fishing with me."

That was something, the thought of being Dad's partner. The two seasons I'd already had on the Banks I'd never gone out in the dories, just stayed on board the vessel and waited to dress down the fish the men brought in. Now I could be out in the dories with Dad and my brothers. When me and Dad come back to the house I found Mom and I told her I was sorry for losing my temper, and that I'd watch my mouth better, and she just held me to her, and I gone up to bed feeling washed clean.

The very next it was, Dad and me rowed out in a dory, just fishing in and around Tarragon, watching the wind and not getting too far off of the island. It was fine and we caught a lot of cod that first day, and a few haddock. Dad was giving me advice on baiting the hooks and using the gaff and all that, and the days went that way, the cold wind cutting our hands open to the bone, and the wind scrubbing down our faces till they shone like old leather. Some sunsets we had those months, like acres of red maple planted in the sky, and Dad would sing hymns, and I'd sit and listen and watch. As June come on, and the sun shone longer, I got to feeling pretty good about God again, what with the wind and the distances and the rhythm of it all. I was wrong to let myself get lulled, but that's how it come out, and I guess Dad hoped that's where I'd fetch up.

Captain Himmelman wouldn't of tried me as a doryman but for Dad speaking up for me. I remember that day on the docks at Lunenburg, the oxen all around us, and their carts full of salt and rope and food, and Himmelman coming over and asking to see my hands, looking for the callouses. He wasn't but a scrap of a man, I was near tall as him by then, but he put the fear of God in me. He looks at me with these dried up little eyes all rimmed in yellow, like raisins setting in old cream, and he says, "Your father tells me you been fishing this winter and spring with him. Says you're done with being our header, you want to sign on as a doryman."

"Yes, sir," I answers him.

"I know your father to be a good fisherman. What do you think you are?"

"I'm my father's son," I says.

Don't that get Himmelman. He had a laugh like he was trying to clear a bone out of his throat and I thought he was choking. He put an arm as sharp and lean as a whip around me and he says, "Boy, you sail with me, and you catch half as much fish as your father, and I'll come back in a rich man." And he went on choking again, and that was it, I was in.

You want to have seen Lunenburg Harbour the day the fleet was heading out. Masts thick as the pine trees on Tarragon. A coming and a going of people, and a lot of women and kids at the dock. I was excited that year because I was going out to do a man's work, I was going out to haul trawl with my Dad.

The *Heather B Sarty* was a trim boat, a long knife blade cutting at the water. She could move pretty quick. She'd shiver under you when the wind first grazed her sails, and I'd think I was on the back of a bird shaking itself and loosening up its wings. Redwis Cross was a good helmsman, and he threaded her out and past Cross Island, just up by the lead vessels. That day was very fair, and the wind was good and steady as I remember it, so Himmelman gives her a full press of canvas. She takes it and runs with it. I was grinning and trying to get near the bow so's the spray would hit me in the face, and didn't I get a big wave soak me through, and didn't the men laugh. Himmelman's looking at me and he yells, "That's what you're in for, doryman, a wet arse and a hungry gut." But I stayed up there by the bow until they called us down for lunch.

The cook weren't Mom, but he weren't so bad either, it was a lot better than gnawing raw bait. You always heard stories from some other boats, so if you had a half decent man you kept him, and you ate whatever come at you. It used to be, on my first two trips, I always sat and ate with the other kids of the dress gang, the throater and the flunky, or off by myself. My first year out I'd gone with Captain Ben Corkum on the *Margaret Demone* as a header, and there'd been no one I knowed on board, and I was only eleven. It was pretty lonely, and when it come time for dressing the day's catch they worked you till you dropped. It weren't a lot of fun that trip, no, and I asked Dad could I go out with him the next year when I was twelve. He said Himmelman would take me on as a header, so that's what I done. But I was still only on the dress gang and I still ate my meals away from the others, away from the real working crew. It was a big difference for me now, this my third trip, and I'm sitting and eating with my Dad and my brothers, a fisherman.

There were twenty-four hands on board the *Heather B Sarty*: Himmelman, who always stayed with the vessel, two kids about ten or eleven who came along as the dress gang to gut and clean the fish, the cook, and the working crew, twenty of us who took ten dories over the side.

My brothers had all been working out of the dories for years. Jonathan Daniel, the oldest at twenty-one, was something of a leader on the boat. He was strong and dark as an oak, but with a joke and a smile for everything. He was the big reader in the family, always a book about volcanoes or the stars or different species of birds tucked into his bunk. Joshua, the next oldest at nineteen, kind of doted on Jonathan Daniel. If Jonathan Daniel made a joke, Joshua had to come up with one too. If Jonathan Daniel was thumbing through a book on the planet Jupiter, you could bet you'd see Joshua with it next. Not that the two had anything much in common. Joshua's jokes never went over and the men thought of him as mouthy. Nobody took him for a leader and this frustrated him, made him bully the younger boys a bit. And you could tell from talking with him that none of those books of Jonathan Daniel's he read sunk in past his eyeballs. New men that came on the *Sarty* never figured Joshua and Jonathan Daniel to be related, for there was Jonathan Daniel, tall and a clump of black hair and a good grin, and Joshua next to him, short and hefty like he'd been chopped out of a block of wood, fine blonde hair blowing back over his ears, squinting and smirking at you like he were one notch above.

The twins hung around together in the same way, the difference being they was suited to each other. Both were quiet, both were thin, both were dark-haired, both were freckled in the summer. The only thing you might of picked up on, whatever Aaron was, Matthew was that little more, not because he tried to be, it was just there in him. He was a bit quieter, a bit thinner, a bit more preoccupied. His smile was a tiny splinter of the lips. But it's not like you never noticed them. They worked hard, when they spoke their voices was firm and steady as taut line, and they both had these green eyes, eyes lit from inside, Grandma Fitch used to say when she was alive. It was queer to look at these eyes and I think it kept other people away from them.

Our family ate together, roamed around each other on the deck, at night we pretty well slept together. It weren't easy being a tall man and having to sleep in them little bunks, and most of my brothers was tall or getting there. I was still all right, but Matthew and Aaron had grown too much that winter, after turning seventeen, and the days was past when they could lay themselves out on the blankets and just stretch for all they was worth. They was banging their ankles and shins and muttering to themselves and trying not to curse so's Dad would hear it. Joshua was short, but Jonathan Daniel was already as tall as Dad, yet this gave him no trouble, he was used to the bunks. He'd get himself into some position and be gone in a couple of minutes. And Dad was, you know, reading by the light of a candle.

I don't know how long he'd do it, because I always fell asleep first. The year before when I'd come on board as a header, this used to make me feel safe, Dad awake in a bit of light and my eyes closing. But now, him reading that Bible, this just filled me with anger and fear. Grandpa Fitch had been drowned and Uncle Tremaine had been drowned and I felt sure that more of us was going to be drowned and that God was the one with the power of life and death. I looked at Dad's face in the light and it seemed to me the Bible was pulling him into some kind of hell.

I remember pleading with him later on in the trip to stop reading it and he says to me, "Look, boy, if it were another book I'd do what you ask, it wouldn't matter to me. But this is the Word of God. God's talking to me here. I can't turn my back on that for anyone."

"The Bible blinds you, Dad," I says. "You seen the Chute boys go under the same as me."

"That weren't nobody's fault. That's just the way a life is. You live a little bit more, you'll see that. It's wove right in."

"God done it, Dad. He's got the sea. He goes after people. He's always done that. The Bible's full of it."

We was resting a bit from setting out our trawl when all this come up, and Dad sat back and looked away from me out over the water. Didn't say nothing to me again till we were bringing up the fish and then he says over his shoulder, "Cale, you see if Missus Chute don't find it's God gives her peace when she gets the news. Nobody else can do that for her. Turn that over and see if you aren't selling him short.''

Selling God short. After what he done. All of us there watching the Chute boys come in with their dory full of fish, and they're pulling, and laughing, and near to the risings with haddock and cod, and we's just about to bring them up, and a wave pitches right into them and pulls them under. The sea was as smooth as blackstrap, and this wave come in all by itself, nothing before it or after it, no swell, and I'd like to know how it come to be there just then. Another minute and we wouldn't of even noticed it. No, but she come in then and done the work she were made to do. There wasn't even time for them boys to call out. The dory was heavy with fish and she went down straight. Some dead cod floated up, but nothing else. I was just shaking and gone cold, and I seen that them winter sunsets and Dad's hymns out in the boat around Tarragon had been nothing but smoke. I seen it plain right then and I never forgot it.

God never let up. It was another morning late in the season we was in the dory heading away from the vessel when the fog come down, and pretty soon Dad had gone, and there I am and this eye of a halibut looking up at me from between my feet. And when Dad's voice come, it was like it come from over my head.

"All right, boy," he says, "we just sits and waits for her to blow the horn."

But the *Heather B Sarty* never did blow the horn, or anyway we never did hear it, for they say she blowed it for two hours or more. After some time, Dad said we should put our backs into her and so we did that, Dad praying out loud that we'd find the vessel. It was a long while, and for all we knowed we was rowing away from the boat, and nothing to hear but the grinding of our oars in the locks. Dad says, "Let's fire the fish over," and it's like he's talking to me from out in the water somewheres. So we throws all the fish we had over the side, three or four hundred pounds, and for awhile it did make the rowing seem easier. But after another hour it felt like nothing was happening and that we were just churning around the inside of some pewter bowl. The muscles in my back were snarling up like bad rope, and every stroke this chunk of pain worked its way deeper and deeper between my shoulder blades, and my whole neck was going stiff.

We stopped once and drank from our water jugs, and I says, "Dad, I don't believe I can keep this up."

"Just another hour, Cale," he says to me, like he's at my shoulder. "You keep her up for an hour and we'll come onto the *Heather B.*"

"What if we don't?"

"We will. I been praying about it. I feel sure we'll see her soon."

So I didn't say anything more, you could see he was set about it. We went at the oars again, and now these long flaps of skin were peeling off my palms, and some strokes you had to bite through your lip to get the pain somewhere else, your hands were stinging so bad. My face, it's like it's right by a kerosene flame, and I starts rowing out of rhythm with Dad. Then I can't even keep my own oars going together, and pretty soon I'm crouching there at the bottom of the boat where it's reeking of blood and dead fish.

Now, when the *Heather B* come up, it come up like a big rock hissing out of the white, jumping right out at us, cracking our side and opening us up. I started sinking and I didn't care, I let myself go, but someone got an arm around me, and there was a lot of shouting all around us, and there's Jonathan Daniel shoving this mug at me, and it's burning my mouth. "Drink it, damn it," he's saying, and I did, and I tell you, it was like they'd made a woodstove out of me. Hot! Why, they had me in some kind of sweat. They put rum and brandy and pepper and God knows what else in that coffee, and it pretty near killed me. They gets me in my bunk, and before I pass out I hear Dad saying, "Thank God," and I mumbles to myself, "God, if you'd had your way of it, we'd be dead now," and that's what I told Dad later. He tells me, "It weren't the boat that saved us, it was the touch of the Master's hand. He laid that sea as smooth as a slick of oil."

"Dad, I rowed my hands off, and I rowed my back off, and it was the two of us got us in the way of the *Heather B,* not God."

"Cale, there was wind and waves when that fog first rolled in. We start rowing for the vessel and all of a sudden it comes calm. What do you make of that?"

"I don't make nothing of it. What do you think Zwicker and Selig made of it? Was you thanking God for bringing them in safe too?"

There was another dory lost in the fog when the *Heather B* come onto us, Ted Zwicker and Frank Selig. It gets on to night, and the fog's still good and thick, and they ain't found them, so they drops anchor. Dad and me are asleep in our bunks by this time, and the boys have just gone below for a bit of supper. It's all of a sudden, as Joshua tells it, there's a loud, slow knocking goes through the whole vessel. Redwis is the one yells down for the captain and everybody piles out on deck. A good bit of wind had sprung up, and the sea's throwing this dory right up against the hull like a maul. She was overturned, and they ties onto her painter and starts hauling her up. Zwicker and Selig's arms and legs drop out of the bottom of the dory and they're dangling there. Joshua says they almost let the dory go. They had a torch lit, and the further up they bring the boat the better they can see Zwicker and Selig wedged under the thwarts and hanging out all stiff and shiny and black in their oils. The light's cutting these shapes into their faces so there's nobody feels it's them anymore.

We laid them in salt and brought them into Lunenburg, and that was four men gone, and the trip back weren't nothing like we'd felt heading out. Zwicker and Selig was both Lutherans, so it was the Lutherans buried them, and Dad made me go to the funeral. It was already October by then, and the wind chopped at us as we stood by the graves. I shut out whatever the minister said and kept to myself on the walk back into town.

The next day we sailed our dinghy up past Bushen's Reef and around the headland into Mahone Bay and Tarragon. After we'd finished bringing the dinghy up the landing, Jonathan Daniel says, "Boy, give me a hand with the sail," and we put it away in the boat house, and he says to me there, "You want to go out with us next year you better smarten your mouth up some quick." He was right about that, because Dad had me down to the fish store the next evening and he went on about respect for the sea and respect for God. He kept hinting about me being too young to understand what had happened to the four men who drowned, how it was easy for a boy to get it all wrong. So I made up my mind right there that I wasn't going to say anymore to Dad about how I really felt about God. I knowed for sure God was going after our family, and that if I wasn't out on the *Heather B Sarty* with Dad and my brothers, I could lose them all without having a chance to warn them or save them.

So I stopped asking questions and went back to singing hymns, and I even made a show of reading the Bible they gave me for Christmas. I could see they noticed all this and that they was pleased. Hank come over on my fourteenth birthday and he took me for a walk to the cliffs on the east end of the island. There were some good waves that day, breaking high up the rock, and we watched them, and he says to me, "Cale, this is what it is. Your father's set on you becoming a minister and he wanted me to talk to you about it. We're looking down the road some, I wouldn't want you getting into it too much before you was eighteen. But it's something you got to work over between now and then. It's a big calling. Your father says you been coming on with your Bible reading and your praying this winter."

I was quick enough to say, "Yes, that's so," but inside it was like I'd been hit by a sea, I was cold and confused.

Hank puts that round face of his close to mine, and he tells me, "Don't worry about it, boy. You got years yet. Tell your father you're turning it over and it'll go well enough. I'll let you alone."

He heads back through the trees and I sits there a long hour, but do you think I could come up with anything? You might of knowed Hank's sermon that night would be James and John leaving their fishing and their father, and going after Jesus. He didn't mean anything bad by it, he thought I was pretty well set to go, just young and scared. Dad had told him that God had ahold of my life, that this young Saul was going to stand for God now, not against him. All that I done by playing my game was to make things worse.

We gone out fishing again that winter, two or three times a week, just Dad and me, and he'd ask questions about the Bible, you know, where was King David born, what kind of gift did Solomon ask for from God, what were the Beatitudes, what places did Paul sail to on his first missionary journey, all this here. I was up reading that Bible some you, I had to be ready for whatever Dad come up with. Now, don't he leave early that year on a frozen bait trip, and my brothers with him, and me left with Mom, and she, why, she keeps it right up. Not a moment of peace. Name the books of the Bible in order. Name the churches in Revelation in order, and what Jesus said to each of them. I'd try and get out to the woodpile right early, we're talking four in the morning, and not come in for breakfast till ten if I could get away with it, just so's to cut down on the time I spent with Mom. She'd push a bowl of oatmeal at me, and sit down with her big brown coffee mug and say, "How are your arms, Cale?"

"I'm doing fine out there, Mom," I'd say, "but there's a lot more to do. I'll get back at it just as soon as I've had my breakfast."

"Don't rush, boy. Your food needs time to digest. Now, you been keeping up with your Bible reading?"

"I been working at it. But I get sleepy and then I have to stop."

"Well," she'd say, "let's find out how you did," and she'd pull this Bible quiz book over towards her, and with one hand she's holding onto the coffee mug, and with the other she's running her finger down the page. One time I did so badly she says, "Cale, I believe you're too much at that wood. Why, at the rate you're going, we'll have to keep the woodstove burning full right through the heat of the summer to get that stacking down some. I want you back in the house by three o'clock every afternoon, and you'll be reading the Bible with me in the parlour."

So that's how it ended up, me sitting there reading the Bible to Mom every afternoon from three o'clock to six. And Mom would nod off too, but if I seen that and stopped reading, her big brown head would come up sharp, and she'd say, "Keep at it now, boy, keep at it, you're doing us both good," so I'd find my place and get going again. It wasn't like she was right hard though. She figured I was grateful for all the extra time she was giving me to read God's Word.

She come and sat on the edge of my bed one night just after she'd finished some baking, and she had that good smell of heat and bread on herself, and patches of flour on her maroon sweater. She leans over me and strokes my face with her hand, and she says, "Cale, you done your father and me some proud. I don't believe there's any of the other families can say they's raised a boy going to go into the ministry. Your grandmother prayed that there'd be one of her grandchildren go to the mission field or get a church here in Nova Scotia. Here it comes down to you, the last one, and her prayer gets answered. You're my baby, but you're coming to be a man of God."

God knows what she tells Dad when he comes back a month later for Easter, but it's out in the boat we are for a bit of a row and he asks me, "Cale, when was it you gave yourself to God?"

"Why," I answers, pulling on the oars, "not so long ago."

"Was it before your birthday then?"

"Oh, I guess so. Just after Christmas, I think."

When we get in he writes it down in his Dad's Bible: Cale Fitch, saved, December 27, 1923. And he sends Hank around to me the very next Sunday, and Hank asks me if I don't want to get baptized before the spring fishing trip, and I tells him that would be all right with me. So he does it that evening, just off of the landing. It was sunset and the sea was glittering like a woodfire, but oh, the water was ice.

"Who do you say this Jesus is?" asks Hank in a loud voice, his door knob eyes big and bright.

"He's my Lord and Saviour," I says to all the persons standing at the shore.

"According to your profession of faith," says Hank, "I baptize you in the name of the Father, and of the Son, and of the Holy Ghost."

He puts me under, and I was sort of scared, I thought something powerful would happen, that maybe God would punish me, or that maybe he'd speak to me, or that I'd see Jesus' face, so I kept my eyes open, but nothing come of it. This disappointed me, as I remember. I'd been feeling bad about fooling the family into thinking I loved God, and the truth of it was I did want to feel good toward God. I wanted to believe in a kind God again, I wanted to walk around Tarragon talking to Jesus and throwing stones at the water. I was already tired of fighting God. I wanted peace. I sat up in my bed that night, trying to talk with him, hoping he'd show me something, anything. But nothing happened and I just got angrier and angrier that he wouldn't say anything a'tall to me. I felt like he was mocking me. So I swore to myself long before dawn come that I would treat God as poorly as he'd treated me. From then on, anything would go, it was a war.

This whole thing about becoming a Christian, I played it to the hilt. Most everybody respected me for it except maybe Joshua, who made a joke about it everytime Dad and Mom weren't around. It was almost like he saw it weren't for real and this used to irritate me. But the stunt kept me in Dad's good graces, and it made it so's I was there on the *Heather B Sarty* for our family's first spring trip. I meant to keep Dad and my brothers from God's splitting knife.

But I found out this weren't so easy. The Banks was messy that spring, fog and snow and slop ice, but we had to get some fishing in, so we'd count our strokes going back and forth in the dory from our marker buoys. We'd been fishing maybe four days and two of the boats never come in for mug-up. This is still early in the afternoon, but I sees that Himmelman's thinking of the men he lost the year before, and he says, "Cut the cable," and Redwis gives it a shot with the axe. The *Heather B* jumps forward and we're racing down to where the boats ought to of been. We picked one of them up right off and that gave everybody a lift. But we never did find the other boat and that was hard, hard for Dad, hard for all of us. It was Jonathan Daniel and Joshua was in that boat.

We blew the horn and we were back and forth looking for them until night come. Finally, we used a spare cable and iron and dropped anchor. I lay in my bunk going from fear to anger and back again, and I seen Dad had turned his face to the hull, I believe he never moved from that position till we got up at two-thirty. There was no talking, and Dad never spoke, never looked at no one while we had our tea and coffee, but it's when we're down baiting up our trawl he says to me, "Cale, you pray now as hard as you ever done. God has a way of hearing the prayers of those that is just been saved, it's like they're his youngest children. You pray and we'll see your brothers back safe." We go over the side and lay the trawl four times that day, and the weather weren't too bad, some sun come through, the clouds looking like a bunch of torn sheets, but the boys we kept on lookout never seen a thing. It's while we're dressing and salting down the catch that Dad asks me, "You been praying, boy?"

"Yes, Dad," I says.

"Something'll come up," he tells me, laying a huge cod wide open with a strong cut.

That night he's back to reading his Bible before bed. He looks over at me once and he says, "I don't see you reading your Bible out here, Cale."

"I find it hard to read before bed," I says. "I get tired."

"That's all right. I guess you'll do some reading on Sundays?"

"Yes, I will," I promises, and he goes back to his Bible, and I goes to sleep seeing the light of the candle all over his face.

It's almost two months we're out. Of course, Jonathan Daniel and Joshua never show up, their boat would of drifted a long way off by then. Dad starts looking worse and worse, he's not sleeping, and he only drinks his coffee and has a few biscuits at mug-ups. At the end he's not reading his Bible anymore, and he says to me when we're hauling up our trawl for the last time, "I never thought he'd do this, Cale."

"Dad," I says, "you got to get it out of your head that it's something against you. It's just something that happened. God ain't out to get you."

"I don't know. I heard some stories about my Dad. It's hard to say what's going on."

"No, Dad. It ain't hard. It's an accident here, an accident."

"That's what I tell your mother, is it?" he snaps at me. "An accident? That'll do her fine?"

And he talks no more to me, not once on the trip to Lunenburg, though I saw him speak with Matthew and Aaron two or three times. It's when we're back at Tarragon, Mom with her apron to her face, that he says, "I got no faith to give you, Mother. You'll have to go to Cale for that."

There's maybe a week, ten days to the summer trip, and Dad spends it sitting in his chair in the parlour, not reading his Bible, but just staring, and then he's working at a bit of wood with a knife, not making anything out of it, just whittling it down to a few scraps and shavings that go all over the carpet.

"You got to say something to your father," Mom tells me, "he'll kill himself going on like this."

"He won't talk to me," I says to her.

"It doesn't matter he talks to you or not. You just talk to him."

So I done that once or twice every day for a week. Told him all the things he'd told me when it come to Uncle Tremaine's drowning, or the Chute boys, or the death of Ted Zwicker and Frank Selig. After a couple of days of this he says to me when I come into the parlour, "Look, here's our Cale, our boy of faith," and this sneer on his face, something I never seen from him before. One day I'm talking and I seen his hands tighten up, and he says, "Get out of here before I lay into you," and I get out of that room right quick, I tell you. But I come back that evening, and he listens to me for maybe ten minutes, and he says, "Thank you, Cale, that'll do fine," and he goes to the bedroom without another word.

The next day I'm reading the Bible to him, and he smiles and tells me, "Cale, I believe we'll see your brothers for supper here come Saturday night."

"Dad," I says, "I would guess they're gone by this time."

"No, it'll be supper this Saturday night. God bless you for sticking in there with me. God bless you, boy."

And he gives me this hug and he's out to the kitchen to talk to Mom.

You might wonder why I ever said the things I did to Dad, standing up for God and all this here. But I seen when this mood come over him that I could work it so Dad would realize how it had to be God's fault. All I had to do was keep at him with his own arguments about how innocent and powerless God was everytime something went wrong. I counted on him getting fed up with this kind of talk, seeing it for the crock it was, and turning against God for good. It would have worked too, even with this crazy notion about Jonathan Daniel and Joshua showing up for supper Saturday night, except that's what they did. There's this knocking at the door Saturday afternoon, and it flies open, and in burst Jonathan Daniel and Joshua. Mom's shouting, and Dad's hollering, and us boys coming down the stairs like a bunch of horses. I didn't give a damn just then about my war with God, I just let Jonathan Daniel pick me up, and I stuck my face into his shirtsleeve so's he couldn't see me crying. And then Joshua's throwing me around till I'm red and laughing hard, and Mom all over the pair of them, why, we was nothing more than a mess of arms and elbows and heads and hair.

They was lean and full of beard, it was like they was a lot older and their eyes a lot darker. We finally gets down to the table and Jonathan Daniel says, "It's the cold was the worst. We had a couple of water jugs, but neither of us thought to pack in a bit of rum. We'd set the trawl, and was just taking it easy, it couldn't of been more than ten minutes. Joshua takes a look and he says to me, 'Jonathan Daniel, I don't believe I can see the buoy,' and we paddled about some, but we never did find it, and by then we'd got ourselves all crossed up in that fog. So we sits and waits a bit, but all it does is start to snow and we needs to get rowing to keep warm, so we goes at her, praying maybe we'll head the right way. But it come night and we was still lost. That compass weren't worth a darn. We ate some of the fish raw, and it got so cold, but we wouldn't let each other fall asleep. First we fires most of the fish over the side, then we rows some, and then we kicks our feet up and down and slaps our hands on our chests, and we makes a kind of game out of it.

"The dawn come like clear fire, and we could see in every direction, but there was no sign of the vessel. Why, there weren't even any gulls. We sets to rowing again, slow and easy, and it gets our blood going, and the sun warmed us a bit too. But by night we was done in and we knowed we had to get some sleep, cold as it was. So what do you think? We wraps ourselves up in each other's arms, oh yes, like a couple of lovers, you. It done fine, but Joshua's beard scraped a lot, and then this grinding of his teeth! We come through the night, and we had a bit of fish left and we ate it, even though it was going bad.

"We goes at the oars again, slow and easy. And pretty soon it's night coming on and back to Joshua's arms, oh my, it was like I got this cod up against my face, that fish had made his breath so bad. We slept off and on, but at least we was warm. It went on like this, I believe, for just over a week, and that's four days without food now. We was still rowing, but not much, maybe a couple of hours a day in bits and pieces.

"Well, one time it's getting on to night, and Joshua comes over to me, and we wraps our arms around each other, and it's just a little bit of warmth we got, and we're laying back like this, and that's how a Yankee boat finds us. They thought we was dead, they thought we'd curled around each other and gone stiff. I tell you, they picked us up and brought us into Gloucester, and in Gloucester they filled us full of food and drink and sent us on to Boston, and in Boston they filled us full of food and drink and kept us in some hospital near a month, and then we kicked up a fuss and got out, Oh, they was grand, but they didn't know where to stop. There was a steamer going to Halifax and we got on her, and then it was this fellow driving out to Lunenburg. It's Vern Langille just sailed us out here. It felt some good coming up from that landing again. I don't care if I never sees a dory again."

Well, but they did though, and it's only three days later. Himmelman couldn't believe it, had to tell two new men their places were taken. He's got one thin arm around Jonathan Daniel's waist, another around Joshua's, and he's looking up at them, and he's saying, "Boys, I tell you what it is. We got ourselves a lucky ship. Come October we'll be heading back in so full of fish we'll be nailing cod to the masts."

Jonathan Daniel and Joshua gets aboard the *Heather B*, and there ain't a man doesn't shake their hands, and you can feel the boat sort of lift up, the crew sees them as a kind of sign. But it was only meant to draw us off. The first day out on the Banks it was, we lost a man.

It's Bernie Rhodenizer come in alone, and he climbs up onto the deck, and we come around him, and he tells us, "One minute I'm there talking to him, and I says, 'Axel, remember that halibut near broke your arm getting him in the boat last spring? I believe it's the grandaddy of them all I'm hauling up here. You get the gaff ready.' He gives a laugh and he starts moving toward me, and he bends down to pick up the gaff, and I seen him slip, and curse, and he goes over. Straight down, I guess. I let the halibut go. I didn't give a damn for it. I don't know, it seems like we can't go out on the *Heather B* anymore without there's somebody drowning."

"We had some good fishing off of this vessel," says Himmelman. "Every now and then, the sea comes for payment. That's how she settles it."

"Yes," agrees Dad, "that's the way of it. The sea's a deep thing, and there's a lot of old rage in her. She's too proud. I hate to see Axel go, Bernie. He was a good father, weren't he? Them kids of his is always at the docks when we come in. That's a hard scratch."

I wanted to yell at them, tell them the sea weren't nothing, that it was God made it and set its ways, but I kept quiet. I had to stay on the boat, I couldn't have my Dad taking me off of it. Himmelman looks over at me, and there we're all bloody and full of slime from dressing down the catch, and he says, "Boy, it's you wants to be a minister. Why don't you give us a prayer here for Axel?" So that's what I had to do. I don't recall what I prayed, but Dad says to me that night, "That was fine, Cale. He's got his hand on your life."

So it got around the whole crew that I was going to be a minister. Not even my brothers knowed anything about it. Matthew and Aaron was some excited, their eyes flickering when they come and told me they was proud of me wanting to serve the Lord that way. But then, they always took after Mom and Dad when it come to religion. You got the feeling when we said grace at the table that they really prayed along with Dad, that they meant it, where Jonathan Daniel and Joshua and me were just going through the motions.

I expected I'd get a fair bit of ribbing from Joshua and Jonathan Daniel about wanting to be a minister, but no, it never worked out that way. Both of them had changed since they got lost in the dory. Joshua didn't swagger as much and he stopped trying to imitate Jonathan. He kept his mouth shut and just done his work, and his work was the work of two men. The only thing he says to me was, "Boy, I sure hope you know what you're getting into."

Jonathan Daniel, he weren't the joker no more. Now you seen him standing at the bow on Sundays, watching the water and the sky. Joshua shaved his beard off when we got to the Banks, but Jonathan Daniel never done that, just let it go. His arms was long and gristly, his face raw with wind. Then you got his eyes coming at you like a blowing sea. I started calling him Elijah for a joke.

It's one night he takes me on deck, and it's when we was sailing for another fishing ground, the jumbo and foresail are up over us like white bone. Redwis is at the wheel and he gives us a nod, but Jonathan Daniel wants me alone, he takes me forward to where the *Heather B* is going at the sea like a wolf. The foam was white and thick, it's like we was stripping back the dark. I felt a surge go through me and I says to Jonathan Daniel, "We're more powerful than the sea."

"I tell you what, boy," he says, "that last night Joshua was asleep against my chest I was looking around me at these whitecaps coming up with the breeze. I'm thinking, 'If one of these drives into us, we're done.' And they starts breaking all around the boat, and when they breaks, they breaks fire. All that spray was nothing but flame, the air was full of sparks. It seemed like the sea was all fire underneath, that it was just throwing this fire off, some big furnace going at her. I guess this went on for most of the night, but no wave ever broke into the boat. And I never felt any heat, but I could count every hair on Joshua's head, that's how bright we're talking.

"I been turning that night over a long time. You know what I think? That it's all fire, every bit of it, the sea, and the night, and all the land and the rocks. Look at the stars burning. And then there's the sun. You get a flame started, everything goes into it, eveything turns back into fire. Wood, grass, and crops, even a man will burn. You take a pile of rocks and you get a fire hot enough, you can melt them down, and you can melt down gold and silver and iron. You remember the night Dad calls us out on the porch and the whole sky is full of green and red and orange? And that picture in one of my books of a volcano blowing up? I guess the belly of the earth is full of fire, and there's fire running right through everything like blood. The air burns too. You put a jar over a candle and it's out. It burns the air to keep going. You see what I'm saying? It's all fire, everything out there is fire. I'm wondering, what keeps us from burning up? The only way I can see it, something holds the fire back. Some kind of god."

All the time he's saying this, the wind gets colder, till our cheeks and ears are burning with it. "This your cold fire, is it?" I asks.

He smiles at me. "Yes, boy. The breaking waves, the moon, wind. They burns like that."

"Weren't you scared?"

"When I seen the waves breaking? Or when I thought all this here out? I was scared both times. The first time I was just scared at what I saw. Now, I'm scared of the kind of strength that can keep it all in. What kind of thing is this, this god that holds back flame? That's why I'm telling you. You sure you want to get close to this? How do you know what it'll do to you?"

"I don't know. It's something Dad wants. I'll work at it for a bit and see what happens."

"Look, boy, I thinks a hell of a lot of the old man. But he's on the wrong tack with this thing. This ain't no person we're talking about, this ain't no human being. This is something stronger and brighter than fire. Now, how do you talk to something like that? How do you pray to it? It ain't got ears and eyes and feet. You know what I'm saying? Some day Dad will find he's got his hands full and he'll be lucky if he can get clear in one piece. I want you to think about this, boy. Why don't you just let it be and stick with us on the Banks here? Why do you want to get close to this thing? This is a god. And a god'll just pull you into itself."

We stands there then, and we looks back at the wake, and it's like it's burning now too, it's like the boat is laying down a strip of bright glass. I get to feeling so lit up, so out in the open there, so seen, I says good night and heads down below, just catching Redwis' face out of the corner of my eye, not much more than a flicker of white. Jonathan Daniel, he stays there at the bow, and for all I knowed he stayed there the night.

I always wondered if Dad knowed what some of Jonathan Daniel's thinking got to be about God. Jonathan Daniel never said nothing to him, but I think that Dad got wind of some of it just the same. There was a beautiful bright day, all sun and gulls, and we was sailing down from the vessel, laying our trawl as we went, and it was me was standing forward with the stick, paying the line out of the tub into the water, and Dad's sitting back and watching the sail when I seen him scoop up a bit of wave in his hand and throw it into his face, laughing good and free.

"Cale," he says, "look at this here, this blue and shining and these white birds just coasting on the wind. Why would you want to plow the land or crawl around in some mine? Look, boy, it's all there for us, and there ain't no end to it. What kind of name do you give to the person who made it? What do you call him? Somebody that makes sea and light and wind, what kind of person is that? You got your whales and fishes, you got your rocks and coves, what does that tell you about him? What kind of person is it we got here? Give him a name!"

He was a kid that day, wasn't he? I believe the only regret he ever had was God didn't bring him into the world with a pair of wings. He saw them gulls riding down a knife edge of air and he said he believed they had the better of it as fishermen, no hooks and trawls and oars, just speed and sharp eyes. "I'll get a plane," he says, "and I'll do my fishing from the air."

He goes on like this all afternoon, it doesn't matter we're sitting waiting on the trawl or gaffing fish off the hooks. I never saw the like of it. It's when we're hauling up our fourth set though, a hook jumps up at my face as I'm gaffing and catches me just below the right eye. Dad's yanking the line down to himself to rebait the hooks, and he gives her a pull before I can yell out, and don't that hook tear the whole side of my face open. I couldn't even scream, I just fell over on my knees and I'm trying to stop the bleeding with my hands. Dad rips his shirt off from under his oils and he knots it tight over the cut, and he starts rowing for all he's worth. That shirt wasn't nothing but a bloody rag in maybe two minutes, I could feel the stuff rolling down my neck and soaking my own clothes full.

It was over a mile and a half back to the vessel, and what wind there was, Dad had it against him. I come close to passing out before he got me in. Some of the boys was already back, and Redwis was one of them, he laid me out on the deck and went at my face with some new fishing line and a big needle he'd run through the flame of an oil lamp. I tell you, I sat up when he ran that first stitch through. Dad took me by the arms, the cook by the legs, and Himmelman shoves this bottle into my mouth and pours all this rum down my throat. Oh, that got me coughing and squirming, and it was Bernie Rhodenizer grabs ahold of my head, and another man sits on my chest, and here this Himmelman's still draining that bottle into my stomach. I guess I got drunk quick enough and that took some of the edge off of the pain.

Redwis stitched her tight as he could, and they cleaned me up and put me in my bunk. My whole skull was throbbing, the skin on the right side of my face was stretched so tight it felt like they'd pinned it to the back of my neck, I got a fever and started to sweat, my head swelled up like some big squash, and the pain near drove me mad, a pair of sharp knitting needles pricking away at my cheek and eye it was. To top it all of, I wakes up with a hangover, the first in my life, and I gets so sick to my stomach I throw up. It was some time before I went up on deck, maybe a week, and I didn't get back to eating with the others for about ten days. Inside of three weeks I was back out in the dory with Dad. Him and my brothers would sit with me in the evenings while I was getting my strength back. Aaron and Matthew would stay at my bunk the longest, taking turns reading to me, and when I needed water in the middle of the night, it was one of them brought it.

There's a bit of a scar to show for it, but you has to look close, and that right eye slanted toward the ear. Redwiss Cross done well enough, and it was him that come and sat with me as soon as he was done fishing for the day, and he told me he'd been a corpsman in the war. He'd sit on the edge of my bunk, hunched over with his elbows jammed into his knees, talking straight ahead of him as if he was talking to my Dad, except he never come by if he knowed Dad was there. When he'd finish talking, he'd look me full in the face, waiting for some kind of reaction, I guess. His eyes was almost clear, there was a hasty bit of green in them, and he kept pushing back his long curls. His hair seemed matted with dried blood. Even out in the sun. If he was alone with me, and he figured on it lasting for a bit, he'd light a cigarette, but I hardly seen him put the thing in his mouth.

"When I was your age," he says to me one time, "it was adventure I wanted, and I took up the fishing, hoping I'd find it there. My Dad was a teacher, you see, and he wanted me into the books, but that wasn't what I liked, I wanted them writing books about me. Oh, there was a lot more to fishing then, a lot more danger. You been having a time what with all these drownings the last couple of years. Let me tell you, we had vessels going down with all hands, or maybe there'd be one man left in the water to tell the story. Cold! The wind was a lot stronger and sharper then, come at us with both fists. Many's the morning we're going up on deck to find all the rigging shining, and these huge icicles hanging stiff as iron from the booms. How would you feel about dumping the dories over the side in that? We was rowing through ice. You know, if it was cold and calm the top of the sea would be all ice and slush. Why, the cod we was hauling up was froze hard, only started kicking around when we puts the salt to them.

"I wanted a beard some bad. I'd try and try, and one of the old boys would laugh at me and say, 'Here's young pepperface now. The cook's been at him again and dipped his chin in the pepper pot.' Nothing come of it for years, then one spring I'm standing on the docks in Lunenburg, and the old boy comes by and says to me, 'You're new here, ain't you? We could use a strapping lad like yourself. How about signing on with Captain Wentzel?' I turns to him and I says, 'I'm already with him, old man. This is Redwis Cross you're talking to.' Oh, wasn't that something, his eyes going big, and him staring. I'd shot up three inches that winter, put on twenty pounds, and the beard was on solid, full of red.

"That beard made some difference, I want to tell you. You didn't feel the wind was going at your jaw with a length of hemp. There was mornings I'd come in for mug-up and I'm all white, frost in my hair and my eyebrows and my beard. And now that she'd got started, she wouldn't stop growing, that thing. I only shaved her off a couple of years ago. I got this girl and she says it scratches."

All the times he come by for the first while, he talked about being on the Banks when he was younger. Then one Sunday with the others up on deck, he come down and hunched over and started in telling me about the war.

"I told you I was looking for something that was an adventure. So when the war come along I left off fishing and signed up for the infantry. I was still pretty young, twenty-two I think I was when we landed in France. Now there was something for you, boy. The first job I had was burying a bunch of dead Frenchies. They'd been hauled out of some trench and they was covered in muck. I pulls on the leg of one of them and it tears right off, like some rotten tree trunk. The smell near put me under myself. Some of them had these big grubs working out through their eyes and nose, it was a disgusting job. The very next morning we moved into the trench they'd been hauled out of.

"It was full of rats, big hairy buggers with mouldy teeth. We had a thing going, the one that could kill the most rats in a week, we gives him four cigarettes or a chunk of chocolate. I used my bayonet on them. They made life miserable for us, I tell you. One of the boys was sleeping and a rat comes along and eats through his cheek. He thought he was dreaming it. Another fellow lost his nose, one bite. You want to worry about the infection that could set in. I seen a man's leg fill up like a balloon, they had to take it off, all because a rat had taken a piece out of his toe. No matter how many we killed, one week it was seventy or eighty all together, there was a couple of dozen more to go at you. You seen them getting fat off the bodies in the shellholes. They wasn't afraid of us.

"Yes, we wanted to get out of that hole, we was ready to take on all of the Kaiser's army to get out of that hole. That's how we felt then. The rats and the grubs and the muck. The rain would come down thick, and it's like you're walking through this filthy stew to get to another part of the trench. The walls would start caving in, and you was never dry, never free of wet and muck. God knows how we kept our rifles clean. I used to wrap mine in the only good blanket I had left, I'd take the cold and sit there shivering in the water and the mud before I'd let my rifle barrel clog up. The Banks is like some pleasure cruise when you put it up against all of that."

"But you said you was a corpsman," I interrupts him. "When did you do that?"

He comes out with a cigarette then, lights it, but never smokes it, just holds it between his thumb and finger and keeps rolling it back and forth.

"Well, boy. We finally got out of that trench. And there's many wished we'd stuck with the rats. An attack come up after two months in that place, and early one morning our guns start dropping shells on the German lines. The ground is shaking, the sky is red and purple, and all you hear is this sound like when a big sail splits in a storm, an awful ripping, quick and sharp, and then this dead feeling comes into your chest. The officer, it was Harvey Bushen from Barss Corner, he says to us, 'Let's go, boys. There can't be much left of them what with all of this.' And we climbs out of that muck and starts walking, and that sky is like the sun broke, there's yellow fire from one end to the other.

"There was men coming out of the trenches all down the line and joining in the attack. To tell you the truth, I can't remember what it was we was supposed to be doing. They said we done well, and some of the Nova Scotia boys got decorated, but all I can remember is the Germans started dropping shells right back on us, and it was just crazy. There was men dropping everywhere around me, finished. I starts running, and pretty soon it's bullets coming at us, and mud flying all over the place. This fellow ahead of me, I seen the whole side of his face come off, and I just jumps over his body and keeps going, but I was some scared, I couldn't even think who I was or where I was running to. These faces and these spiked helmets come up, and I could see my arms sticking out in front of me with this rifle and bayonet, but it was like I was standing back from the whole thing, it didn't feel like I was in my own body. We took this trench and it was just like the trench we'd left.

"The attack lasted maybe twenty minutes and we spent the rest of the day putting as many bodies under as we could, didn't matter they was German or Canadian. All the time I was digging I felt I was still back from it all. Everything was sharp and clear. I can remember that day better than I can yesterday afternoon. I come across a wounded man, one of ours, and I yells to Bushen, but he says there's no corps-men, a bunch of them got blown up during the attack. So I squats by this man and gives him some water. He starts talking to me about his family in Digby Neck and after a bit I make up my mind to get him to a medical station. Bushen said there'd be one about a mile down the line, so I slung this fellow over my back and I got him there.

"That was a walk. All I saw was bodies, piles of them, and the medical station was the same way, except there the bodies was squirming. I puts this fellow down and they tell me they'll get right to him. It seems like he's got a good chance of making it, so I decides to stick around a bit and see how he does. I light up a cigarette, and I walk behind the tents, and there's a heap of arms and legs they's cut off and that gets me, all of a sudden I'm sick. It made me think of the pile of heads and guts we get when we're dressing down a catch. And these blue and green flies sitting on everything. It was like I come back into my own body right then and I couldn't take what it was going through.

"I walked over to where I couldn't see anything at all and I sat about an hour. Then I thought I'd check up on the fellow I'd brought in and head back. I goes to the tents and I finds him right where I'd put him down, nobody had even touched him, and he was dead.

"'What the hell is this?' I starts yelling. 'I brought this man in over an hour ago and you ain't even looked at him!'

"'All right,' says this doctor, and he's sitting back on a crate smoking a cigarette. 'I'll take a look at him now.'

"'He's dead,' I says, 'you son of a bitch!'

"'Look,' he says to me, 'we've been up to our necks in it all day. We lost a lot of corpsmen in the attack and we just don't have the people to work on everybody properly. I'm damn sorry about your friend but this is the first time I've been off my feet in fifteen hours. When you're curled up in your blankets tonight, I'll still be at it.'

"He goes back in the tent and I just squats and closes the fellow from Digby Neck's eyes. And I walks back to my unit. All night I'm dreaming off and on. I see this fellow looking at me and dying and his eyes hanging open and his skin turning purple and yellow. In the morning I makes up my mind to work as a corpsman. I tells Bushen and I just up and heads back to the medical station with my rifle and my pack. The doctor was sitting on that crate again, but his head's drooping, and his body's bent over sideways, a cigarette burning out right between his fingers.

"I wakes him up and I says, 'Okay, doc. What do you want me to do?'

"He remembered me too. 'Give me your rifle and ammunition,' he says, and I did that. He gives me a red cross armband and he says, 'I'll put you with an ambulance unit. You ever driven a team of horses?'

"'I guess I have,' I tells him.

"'All right,' he says, 'that's what you'll do. There'll be another attack in a couple of days. Until then you can help me here.'

"So that's what I done. I stayed on as a corpsman until the end of the war."

He stops then for a bit, jabs out his cigarette. He turns and looks me in the face and pushes the hair up out of his left eye.

"'Boy,'he says, 'I used to look out over them battlefields after it was done, and I seen the heaps of men's bodies, all black and stinking and full of flies. And I said to myself, 'This is your war and adventure, Redwis. It's no more than a bunch of oxen come through and had a dump.'"

I didn't see him again for a couple of days, but he come in early one afternoon, most of the others was still out hauling up their last set, and he brings me a couple of fresh biscuits from the cook.

"Here you go," he says.

"Thank you, Redwis," I tells him around my first mouthful, for I was some hungry, my appetite was just starting to come back.

He watches me eat for a bit and then he says, "So you're going to be a minister, eh, boy?"

"Yes," I answers.

"I used to have some trouble with this idea of God, a good God," he says, and he looks away, settling his elbows on his knees. "Just like that doctor said, the boys was ordered to attack two days later. We got where we wanted to go, maybe another two hundred yards further on, and then the Germans come back at us and there was this fearful fighting going on in our trenches. The attack broke up, but there was a lot of bayonet wounds, ugly things leaving necks and stomachs wide open. We started bringing the bodies in to the tents and it wasn't long till I was soaked in blood, I had to throw my uniform away and get another. The doctors are trying to stitch wounds as fast as they can and what happens, one of them teaches me how to do it so I can help them out. There's no morphine for these wounded they're piling up next to me, and I got to get another corpsman to hold them down while I try to put them together. They're screaming and biting on rags, and I'm doing the best I can, and half of them are dying anyway. The day's over and I'm still going at it in the light of a candle, and this one fellow is cursing me as I'm working on his throat, and that's how he dies. I goes out for a breath of air and I'm sitting on my helmet and this doctor comes over, the one who took me on as a corpsman.

" 'So?' he asks.

" 'The hell with it,' I tells him. 'We're getting maybe four back out of ten.'

" 'Some days you'll be thanking God for that.'

" 'I'll be thanking God for nothing.'

"He pulls an old crate over and he sits down, and he says, 'The thing to do is not to get upset over this God thing. It just throws you off. There's nothing out there. And even if there is, it doesn't matter. He ain't got a hand in this. We're doing the killing, and if there's going to be anybody coming back from this thing, we'll be the ones doing the healing too. Getting all churned up over what the hell God is doing only makes your job a lot harder. It wastes your energy and you lose your concentration, and in the end it doesn't make any difference God cares or doesn't. It's you puts the stitches in, not him. It's you takes the legs off. It's you goes in with the stretcher. Worshipping him doesn't change a thing. Believing doesn't make any more sense out of it than not believing. The bombs still drop and the bodies keep piling. So what you got to do is realize all this and pull right back. Don't get caught up in it. Don't try and figure it out. Tell yourself, "There's no one behind any of this. It's just men can't get along." Then do your job and try and keep the men alive. It saves you a whole lot of sleep and you end up thinking a lot clearer when you wake up.'

"So that's what I tried to do. The next day there was another attack and bombs going off every place, and bullets, it was a living hell. I drove the horses into a place where the thick of the fighting had just passed, and we get out the stretchers and we fill that ambu-

lance in about thirty minutes. I was about to take the load of us back
to the tents when I seen a man out near a shellhole waving a hand at
me. I jumped down and got ahold of him, the whole of his skull was
pushing through his face, but he was still talking and breathing, and
as I gets him over my shoulder this shell comes crying and blows the
ambulance apart. There wasn't nothing left but wood and mud and
one of the horses screaming. At first I thinks to myself, 'Oh my
God! How could you let this happen?' But then I done what the doctor told me and I said out loud, 'It's a German shell, and it's a war,
and that's where the shell landed. It's a hell of a thing.' And I set off
for the medical station. I got him in and by God, boy, he's alive
today. Makes his home up in New Germany. Now, it's that way of
looking at things got me through the war, and it's got me through a
lot of drowning on the Banks too."

"But there must be a God," I argues with him.

"What the hell does it matter?" he answers me. "It don't change
one thing here, don't make one thing happen differently. Here we
got your Dad with us for how long? A strong Christian, a praying
man. And we still loses men every trip. God don't make a
difference, boy. You got to live out your life without getting tied up
in all this thinking about God. You'll live better for it."

"It don't all just happen by itself," I says.

"How do you know?"

"There's plans out there. You can feel them working."

"Boy, you drive yourself crazy trying to see plans in everything.
How about the Chute boys? Or Zwicker and Selig? What kind of
plan do you get out of that? You going to tell me that's the working
of a good God?"

"No. That's the working of a God hard and full of hate. It's him is
behind everything, it's him is out to cripple every one of us."

"Why, boy," Redwis says, and he's looking at me strange, "what
are you saying?"

"I'm saying he's out there and he kills."

Redwis gets up and he tells me, "You're talking crazy. There ain't
no one out to get any of us. It's just the way things happen."

"No. You take a good look. You'll see what I'm saying."

Redwis leaves in a hurry, as if he were a religious man who
couldn't bear to hear another word of sin. Not two days later a storm

blew up and Himmelman keeps the dories in, the vessel's jogging so hard the bowsprit's under the water every pitch. I didn't have much trouble, but a lot of the others, why, even Joshua and Jonathan Daniel was heaving into buckets. Bernie Rhodenizer goes up on deck for a storm watch and a rogue wave come and picked him up and throwed him against the main mast, smashed his head in. Himmelman and Redwis tried to get ahold of him, but the whole deck was slanting off to the left and Bernie was washed overboard pretty quick.

I come up on deck some time that night. The wind had gone down, though the swells was still high. We was at anchor, moving back and forth with the sea. There's Redwis standing at the stern and I walks back to him. He's got a cigarette lit and the smell of it's right sharp. He don't even look at me, he's staring out over the bit of sea where the moon's spread down.

"Well, boy," he says, "what are you going to tell me about Bernie?"

"I guess God's been wanting him since he took his partner," I answers. "I guess he wanted both of them."

"Now, what if I says to you it was just the storm killed him?"

"God has ahold of the storm or he ain't God."

"But suppose God made the world and then let it be, let it go its ways?"

"No. Too many things fit together too neat. It's like somebody's playing checkers with us."

"A man stands on the deck of a vessel and a wave that's been out there for hours hits the vessel. That's how them things happen."

"It happens too often."

"Lots of men have been saved by the storm. I heard of vessels thrown up onto land so high the breakers couldn't get them and all the crew safe. I heard of men taken over the side with one wave and brought back on with another. That's what happened to Himmelman when he was about your age. Wouldn't your God make dead sure of getting those men?"

"That ain't the way of it. It's part of his game to play with us like that, it's the cat with the bird. He paws us over a bit, takes all the fight out of us, and then he puts an end to us when he likes."

"Boy, it's not God you're talking about, it's death."

"God and death, it's the same thing. There ain't no difference."

Redwis throws his cigarette at the sea like a dart and turns full on me. His eyes are wide, like someone's got their fingers hooked in at his lids and is stretching them back. His face is jerking up and down with the movement of the deck and his skin is like bone in that moon.

"No, boy," he snaps in a loud voice, "I don't believe that. God put it all together and left it up to us. I would say that's fair. We do the best we can and what happens is up to us and a bit of luck. Our bad times ain't nobody's fault. Nobody's coming after us, nobody's scheming. Things fall out the way they do and you put up with it. There's no reason you got to go around living as if God Almighty is got this big war going on against you."

"If that's so," I comes back at him, "it's all the same and God ain't no better than a hammerhead. Making a world full of sea and storms and backing off from it all, knowing it'll be a living hell for us, but not giving one damn about it. How's that any better than what I been saying? Either way he's seeing to it nobody gets out of any of it alive."

"No."

"Oh, by God, yes. If God don't got ahold of death, he ain't God. He works it. He works everything."

Redwis is staring at a square of light on the water that's looking like a piece of crinkled cloth. He jabs his chin at it. "It's like they're putting a blanket over Bernie," he says. Then he looks up at the night. "I don't like hearing you talk this way, boy. It ain't right for someone so young to be full of the things you're saying. I don't believe it's good for any of us. I don't believe it's good for the vessel." And he goes past me and down below.

I never talked with him again until we was heading back for Lunenburg in October. We'd had a good trip, a decent catch of fish, and Redwis had just taken the wheel from Jonathan Daniel. I'd been talking with my brother when Redwis come up, and I was going to go down, it was sunset, but Redwis says, "Let me talk with you a bit, boy," and I knowed what it was going to be.

What had happened a couple of days before, Redwis had fallen out of his dory, but he stayed up until his partner could row over to him. He hauls Redwis in and a shark comes under the boat, gives them a bump, and stays with them the rest of the day. Never fouled their trawl or went after their catch. Just stayed with them.

We're steering into that October sun, and it's falling, like someone's tipped a barrel of Cortlands, and he says, "Boy, that shark never left off until I was standing on the deck. I looks down and I tell you, for awhile it's like we're going at it eyeball to eyeball. Then he tucks himself under and that's the last I seen of him. I been turning it over some.

"When that war come to an end, it was only me and another fellow come out of it from our town. There were thirty or forty others and every one of them got killed. The both of us went back to fishing. He drowned two years ago. The other night I had a dream about the ambulance getting blown up. I come over to look at the bodies and they turns their faces to me, all terrible and ripped up, and they says, 'They were looking for you and they got us.' I don't know. It scares a man, what with all your talk. Most of the medical unit I was with got killed. What do you figure, boy?"

"You know how I sees it."

"I knows. But what do I do about all this?"

"If I could do it, I'd get all of my family off of the sea."

"Oh, no. I'm not talking about that. This is my place here. No, I can't leave the fishing."

"Redwis. If you won't leave the sea, then keep your eyes about you."

"You really think God is that way?"

"Yes."

"Boy, you ain't going on fifteen, you're going on fifty."

He smiles at me then, but that's it. He turns his eyes to the sea and the wheel and he says no more to me.

We're back home a couple of months, it's just before Christmas, and Jonathan Daniel asks me to go out in the boat with him. That's when I find out he was listening to everything Redwis and me was saying.

"Boy," he's telling me, "you know what I said to you. There's a powerful god holds the fire back in this world. You don't mess with a god like that."

"You never said anything good about him," I argues. "You never said he was a god that cared about us."

"That don't mean you go up against him and start calling him a killer. Didn't I tell you not to get close to him? All you're doing with your talk is drawing attention to yourself. You know what it's like to be right close to the fire? Let me tell you something. You was hardly more than a bit of skin when we had a fire in our old shed where Dad kept a couple of hogs. Joshua kicked over a lantern and the straw went up, and he runs out of there and he doesn't tell anybody what happened. Dad and me was down in the fish store, and he was showing me how a gill net worked when Mom started hollering. We runs up there back of the house and that shed's nothing but yellow fire. Hot! I could hear the hogs screaming, and I tries to get in at them, but it's like the heat was tearing my flesh off in strips. Pretty soon both of them comes out of the fire, squealing and rolling and burning, the stink of their burnt hair made you sick. There was nothing we could do. They was covered with blisters and blood. Dad got the rifle and shot them both. The smell stayed on the island for days, enough to make your stomach go over. I never forgot what the heat felt like on my arms and face. You don't want that, boy. I'm telling you, you don't want it."

The sun was out then and it looked like somebody had thrown dimes into the sea. Jonathan Daniel points and says, "Look   w. Ain't that some beautiful? Well, that's because we're at a distance. But you get in close and that sun's fire, and it ain't got no mind of its own, it'll just do what fire does no matter who you are. You stays back and it's fine. You see what I mean, boy? Your mouth has always been getting you into trouble. Put those crazy ideas on God out of your head before something bad happens. That hook tearing your face open ought to have been warning enough."

We never talked about it again that winter. Christmas was a good time. With six of us bringing money into the house we did better than most. We had a ham for Christmas Eve and a goose for Christmas Day. On my fifteenth birthday in January, Mom made a huge cake shaped like a Bible opened up to a verse from Isaiah: "Fear not, for I have redeemed thee. I have called thee by name. Thou art mine."

Dad asks me, "You know the rest of that verse, don't you, Cale?"

"No," I tells him, "I don't."

"Why, 'When thou passest through the waters, I will be with thee. And through the rivers, they shall not overflow thee. When thou walkest through the fire, thou shalt not be burned, neither shall the flame kindle upon thee.' Now, there's a promise, for you, boy."

Mom seemed to want to spend a lot of time with me that winter, always asking me to help her in the kitchen, or to fetch wood and feed the stoves, so I spent less time with Dad out handlining. I remember one morning all of them was out on the water but me, and Mom's rolling dough. She leans on the counter, looking out the window to the sea, and she says, "The summers go too long. I don't know what to do with myself sometimes. I bake a half-dozen loaves, but I eat only a couple of them inside of a week and I end up having to throw the rest away. The birds eat it. I take some time to crumble it up for them. I wish your father would take to just fishing off the island and coming home every night. What does he need to go out to the Banks for? A month on the frozen bait trip, two months on the spring trip, another four on the summer trip. There's plenty of fish here. Oh, he's got something going, I guess. He has to get out there to do it. What would I do if he didn't walk up from the landing with all of you one day? When we thought your brothers was gone I seen I could keep ahold of myself. I don't know as I could do that if it was your father gone. I never seen such a man. Thank God he's my husband. I can't see the Lord doing that to me, taking him away. Almost losing the boys was a hard enough thing. I can't see the Lord putting me through that again, I'd say once is enough for a family. Now, Cale, you'll leave the sea in a few years and I'm not sorry. But if you could watch him, watch your father until then, it would put your mother more at ease. I like to think of you being right close to him. He's so proud of you wanting to be a minister."

"Mom, I fishes with him and I sleeps right across from him. I'm watching him all the time. There's nothing to worry about. I'm not going to let anything happen to him."

She looks at me a long moment, smiles, pushes a bit of hair out of her face with the heel of her palm, and goes to rolling out her dough again.

It was a week after this she asks me if I don't want to go for a walk. This is just evening and we heads up toward the lighthouse. At first it's nothing but talk about how chilly it is, the colour of the sky, the yards of the houses we walk past. She has her maroon sweater unbuttoned and crossed over her breasts like a bath robe, her hands jammed up under her armpits, and her head's down so that I'm looking at the sturdy curve of her hair bun, something that always reminded me of good strong wood spun into a tight bowl. You could hear the sound of our shoes on the gravel path and they got louder as it got darker.

Finally, we finish talking about the lighthouse and Charlie Zinck, the keeper, and she stops at the edge of the trees, and says, "Cale, your brother Aaron has got himself a girlfriend."

"Oh?" I says, because I didn't know anything about it.

Mom looks out over the woods and after a bit she tells me, "He met her in Bridgewater. It was that Christmas party for the Baptist young people he and Matthew went over to. I ain't against him having a girlfriend, and I guess he's old enough to find out what it's like, but I see she's on his mind all the time now. He's always daydreaming. Picks at his food. Now he's talking staying over there with her folks for February and there's so much work to do here."

"Mom. There ain't that much. They're out handlining most of the time as it is. I can take care of the work."

"If I could see her I believe I'd feel better about it. Why doesn't she come over here? No, he's got to go way out to Bridgewater to see her. Aaron's the last one I'd expect to find a girlfriend. He's always kept right to himself. His only close friend is Matthew. Aaron had scarlet fever when he was young and he got quieter and quieter after that. I don't see it's good for him to get more that way."

I starts laughing. "Mom, don't that always happen to a fellow when he's got a girl? I guess Dad got like that when he started seeing you."

"Maybe he did, maybe he didn't. All I know is, Aaron ain't like your father, he ain't got your father's toughness. I seen him moping for days when a cat would die on the island. Never wanted to learn how to use the rifle. I'm surprised your father got him out fishing. He's a frail child. I don't want no girl hurting him."

"I guess he's tougher than you think. He takes in as much fish as anybody, and Matthew told me once how a hook went through Aaron's hand. Aaron cuts into his own hand and gets it out. Now, I think he can handle a girl. I don't think he's going to flop around at her feet. Remember the day he was out with Angus Young?''

Angus Young had taken Aaron handlining a few years before. A seagull had gone for Aaron's baited hook when he brought it up, and the hook caught in the bird's beak. Aaron was some upset, they got the bird close to the boat, but they couldn't calm it down and they couldn't work the hook loose. Angus got frustrated and he took the bird and smacked its head against the hull, broke its neck. Aaron starts yelling at him and asks Angus how he'd like it if somebody beat his head against the boat, and Angus tells him to go to hell. Aaron piles into him, just tackles him, and down they go, fishing lines tangling in their feet and all of it. Aaron gets a few good shots into Angus and this makes Angus furious. He takes a wild swing at Aaron and cracks his fist into the side of the dory. Breaks his hand. Aaron brings the boat in and Angus goes looking for Dad. Dad comes down to where Aaron is cleaning fish at the landing and says, "Let's hear your side of it." But Aaron just turns these green eyes on him, I guess, and he says, "He broke a seagull's neck for nothing." He never apologized for it and I don't believe Angus ever spoke directly to him again. But we all stood back and took another look at Aaron.

Mom remembered and she snorted through her nose a couple of times, her way of trying to hold in a laugh. She hugs me to her and she's strong and warm and smelling of frost and salt cod.

"Okay, boy," she says, "we'll set back and see how it goes. But if I could get a look at her eyes and face I'd feel a lot better."

So Aaron went to Bridgewater for a month and Mom never said another word about it to me. Matthew wasn't that pleased about Aaron going off but I doubt that Aaron even noticed, when he left the island he was practically flying. Dad asked if I'd go on the frozen bait trip with them and I said yes, so Mom was alone early that year, though I counted on Aaron being back soon to help her out. I felt a little bad about it, Mom standing there on the landing as we went out, but I'd never been on a frozen bait trip before and I had to see what it was like.

In the spring and summer trips, we'd usually pick up fresh bait from the Newfoundland outports, but this here was too early for that, we only had frozen bait to use. The Banks was awful. Cold and fog and snow, and we heard later a vessel run over one of her own dories, lost both men.

We had a time of it. It seemed nothing was running for us. Days would go by and all together we'd bring in maybe six hundred pounds of fish. We'd be up early in that ice and wind to set trawl, and then we'd haul her up and nothing, not a bite, so Himmelman would hoist the flag and we'd all head in, sail to another place where not much more was likely to happen. It's a good thing the trip only lasted a month. You could see the boys looking worn out and grim when we'd get up for breakfast. I seen Redwis staring at me once, sitting hunched over a coffee mug. I tries to smile at him but he just looks over my shoulder and sucks in his lips.

That was a hard drill. We come in with a lot less than a quarter of a hold of fish. I think I made twenty cents off the trip. The only thing we had to look forward to was the spring season starting inside of two weeks, with a warmer sun and maybe a lot more fish running. We got back to Tarragon and there's Aaron splitting kindling, a crazy smile on his face.

"What's up?" asks Joshua.

"I'm going to be married," Aaron says.

Oh my, don't we all just hold back and look at him. Dad says, "What are you talking about, boy?"

"Next Christmas," he answers. "In Bridgewater. Her folks is all excited about it. I want to get a place in Lunenburg and keep going out on the *Heather B Sarty.*"

"All right," Dad says. "What does your mother think of all this?"

"She's fine now. I promised her we'd go in to meet Cathy before the spring trip."

"All right, all right. You finish that wood," says Dad, and he heads into the house.

The rest of us are looking at Aaron standing there with the axe and smiling at us. Finally, Joanthan Daniel goes up to him and shakes his hand.

"Congratulations, Aaron," he says right solemn like. "I hope it goes well for you."

"Thank you, Jonathan Daniel. I feel some good about it."

So we all shook his hand, but Matthew kept his head down and then walked off back to the landing. Aaron was going to call him, hesitated, turned back to us with a limp smile, and glanced over all the wood he had chopped. He was about to take up the axe again when Dad come back out of the house and put an arm around him. "Well, let's go see what she looks like," he says. "Joshua, you'll come along and help Aaron and myself with the dinghy. Your mother doesn't take to a boat poorly handled. Jonathan Daniel, you'll stay back and keep an eye on Matthew and Cale. We'll head in for Chester tomorrow. You can figure on us being gone four or five days."

They didn't get away for the next two days though, the wind was churning up the Bay some fierce. Finally, it come calm enough to sail for Chester. From Chester they could make their way into Bridgewater. Matthew and Jonathan Daniel and me did a few chores, cooked a few meals of hodge-podge, took it easy. Matthew went down to the fish store a fair bit and sat there going through the gear. He says to me once, "Cale, I hope she dies."

"Don't talk like that," I says. "You wait, you'll wind up getting along with her. Weren't you always saying you wanted a sister?"

But his green eyes spit light and he tells me, "No. I hope to God she dies."

Jonathan Daniel, he started doing these sketches. They was strange things. There was one of a bunch of gulls flying near the sun. They was made to look as if they wasn't no more than things that had been carved right out of it. Another was of the sea around Tarragon in a storm and it was like the wind was flames and setting the whole ocean on fire. The oddest one had a cross hanging in the sky, and fire from earth streaking up to it, and fire from heaven streaking down to it, and there it's burning like a star in the middle of it all. He coloured that one with some old crayons, put every colour you could think of into that star and its rays. When he shows me that one I asks him, "What is all that?"

His wrist comes out of his shirtsleeve and he puts three fingers on the star, looking at it like he's daydreaming.

"That," he says, "that's the cross in the Bible."

"What do you mean? Do you mean Jesus' cross?"

"I'm not sure. You know how much the Bible says about fire? Moses and the burning bush. God coming to the Israelites at night in a big pillar of it. The chariot of fire coming for Elijah. The angels is always fire. On the day of Pentecost, fire comes down from heaven and starts burning over the heads of the apostles, but nobody gets hurt. It's like they get stronger. I don't know. This picture come to me out there on the rocks. It made me warm when I was drawing it. I still get that feeling whenever I stare at it.''

It was hard not to keep looking at the star. Whenever I did, I felt good about it and bad about it at the same time. You'd start feeling warm, and then you'd feel something was coming together, the whole of everything was tying into that star. But then I'd get another feeling, the same one I got the night Jonathan Daniel told me about the sea breaking into fire, and everything coming out of fire, and a god holding it all back. It was a feeling of being out in the open, of being seen. It was like when I was hiding in the cellar once, eight years old and thinking I was going to get a licking. It was dark and cool and I was huddled up next to the potatoes, feeling right safe. All of a sudden, the trap door flies open and this bright lantern comes into the cellar at the end of somebody's hand. It lit up everything and it scared me some bad. I knowed whoever was coming would find me, I was sure they could see every part of me, and I knowed they'd punish me right there, so I started crying. The star was like that lantern flame coming at me out of the dark.

Jonathan Daniel smiles at me, hardly using his lips, and he says, ''I believe God can control the fire he gives you. I think he can let you get right close to it without it killing you. It's like he lets you get close to the beginning of it all, the first fire that's still burning, putting flame to the whole universe. I believe he'll let that fire touch you.''

I says to him, ''That's not what you was telling me before.''

''No. I been turning it over. I tell you, though, you got to go at this fire right. If you don't, it will kill you. You got to go at it with the proper frame of mind.''

''And what's that?''

''I don't know yet.'' He gives me that scrap of a smile and puts his pictures away.

Mom and Dad come back right pleased about Aaron's girlfriend. I guess she was some nice looking and Mom said she was a hard worker around the house. Her father was a good Christian and ran a general store. Him and Dad got along fine. The two women done less well, but Mom figured as Aaron wasn't marrying the mother things would be all right. The wedding was set for the twenty-third of December in Bridgewater and the pair of them would spend the winter on Tarragon while Cathy's father found them a place in Lunenburg.

We gone down for the spring trip and this time Cathy and her mother's there to see us off. Cathy was nice too, hair as dark as a forest, and her eyes and hands so clean and neat she made me think of good strong waves. Matthew had nothing to say to her, went right on board the *Heather B.* Aaron must of talked to her about it because she pretended not to notice. She said hello to each of us. When she took my hand I looked down and she must of thought something of that, she laughed.

"I guess your brother's afraid of me," she tells Joshua.

"I don't think any girl but Mom's ever touched him before," Joshua says. "There ain't much on the island."

"We'll have to see what we can do for him, won't we, Aaron?" she asks.

"I guess," Aaron answers.

I took off and put my gear on the vessel.

"Who's that girl?" Himmelman asks me.

"That's Aaron's girl," I tells him. "He's going to marry her."

"Ain't that something?" says Himmelman.

Dad come by and asks, "Cale, you going to say good-bye to Cathy?"

"No," I says.

"He's scared," Joshua sneers, coming in with his gear.

"No, I ain't."

"You're afraid she's going to grab you or something?" Joshua asks.

"No. I just don't want to go down to the dock again. Why should I?"

"All right, boy," Dad says. "Do what you like. Joshua, let him alone now."

I daydreamed about Cathy. I thought of her touching me with her clean white fingers, I thought about brushing her dark hair. I had it that she'd be waiting for us when the *Heather B Sarty* come in, and when she's done hugging Aaron and he's helping unload the fish, we goes aside, and she asks, "What did you bring me, Cale?"

I hands her a beautiful conch, or maybe a pearl, or the blade of a swordfish, and she hugs me, and she's soft and warm, smelling like flowers.

"Cale," she says, "I guess we'll have to tell Aaron sometime."

"Yes," I says. "I'll break it to him. He'll be all right. He's got Matthew."

"You're strong," she tells me, and she kisses me at the corner of my mouth. I'd get kind of light-headed thinking all this here. A couple of times Dad would have to give me a poke with one of the oars. "Cale," he'd say, "what are you dreaming about? Get ahold of that trawl line."

I don't know what Aaron thought about, but I had Cathy in my head a long time. After awhile, the only problem I had on my mind was how I was going to tell Aaron about me and Cathy. Should I do it at sea or on Tarragon? Should I have Cathy with me when I told him or should I just talk to him man to man? Should I tell Dad about it first or should I keep it to myself until I told Aaron? This was the way my head was going. I never thought about God at all, or the sea, or the fishing. But that changed pretty quick.

The fishing hadn't got any better than the trip before, there was hardly any cod in the hold and we're into our third week on the Banks. The men was looking paler and paler when they come in for the day. Himmelman must of changed places fifteen times and we still was doing no better. What made it hard, the other vessels wasn't having the time of it we was. One morning the *Mary Stevens* come by us, heading back into Lunenburg.

"What's your trouble?" Redwis calls over to them.

"Our trouble is we got no more room to put the fish," they shouts back. "We got to get rid of this load so's we can get back at her. How's it going for you?"

When this story gets around the vessel the crew starts getting restless and talking. "There's bad luck on this vessel," they're saying, "bad luck sailing with us."

Dad looks up at me one night from his Bible and he asks me, "What do you think, Cale?"

"I don't know, Dad," I says, and I still got Cathy on my mind.

"There was times Peter and the others couldn't get a decent catch, but the Lord got one for them."

"Well, maybe that's what he'll do for us."

"That's what I'm thinking. How about we go at it with some prayer, boy?"

"All right, Dad."

But nothing happened. Not that you'd think God would of listened to anything I had to say, but you'd think he might of done something on account of Dad's praying. But there's another week gone and still no fish to speak of. About the best haul Dad and me ever had that time was a fish to every two hundred hooks, twenty-five cod to show Himmelman when we come in. I don't think anyone done any better. That's the kind of spring trip we had.

We're hauling up the dories one day and there's Redwis come up, the last one. The whole crew is standing on deck wet and cold, and there's no catch a'tall, no one's had a bite. The clouds is low and dirty grey and the vessel is creaking under our feet and no one's talking, we're just watching Redwis climb on board, our hands at our side, seawater staining the wood under our boots. Redwis takes a look around, sees the dress gang standing there with nothing to do, and he says, "I tell you what it is, we got a Jonah on board." The men don't move but you feel a tightening. They watch Redwis turn to me, "And by God, I know who it is. It's this Fitch boy. He's a God-hater and a blasphemer and he's running from judgement, and God Almighty's taking it out on all of us to get at him."

The men start staring at me and Redwis' eyes are on me pale and sharp. I couldn't say anything. I just stared back at Redwis, calling myself a fool for having told him a thing.

"That's enough of that," my Dad says. "Cale ain't been against God for a long time now. He'll be going into the ministry in a couple of years."

"No," snaps Redwis, still glaring at me, "he ain't changed, Mister Fitch. He's pulling the wool over your eyes. It's God Almighty he's cursing when your back is turned."

"No," I finally gets out, "that's a lie. I'm on my knees every night before God."

"That's so," speaks up Wayne Knickle. "I seen the boy. Let him alone, Redwis."

But Redwis gets wilder and he's pointing this finger at me, almost yelling, "We got to get him off this vessel. Drop him off at one of the outports. The sooner we're done with him, the sooner we'll be hauling up fish. I'm telling you!"

"Shut up!" shouts Himmelman. "Are you drunk? Look at you. You ain't shaved, you ain't cleaned yourself up, you ain't changed your clothes. You're disgusting. And then you come out at this boy who's a third of your age. Get out of my sight, man, before I gets my hands on you and throws you into one of them outports. Go on!"

We breaks up and Dad says to me, "I should never of let him spend all that time with you. It's my fault. I always knowed him to be a touchy character. You best steer clear of him, Cale."

Over the next few days there's nothing but a couple of hundred pounds of fish come in, and Redwis has some of the boys sitting close to him at mug-ups. It's one of these nights I'm up for watch, and I'm standing at the bow thinking about Cathy, and there's this blast of white light, and cold, sharp cold going right through me. I felt like I was sinking down into water, hands over my head, just like my dreams about Uncle Tremaine. Then somebody's slapping me in the face and I gets mad. I open my eyes, I'm trying to stand on my feet, and I'm letting go with my fists.

"All right then, Cale," my Dad says and he's leaning his hands on my chest. "It's your father. You fell over the side. You're fine now."

"Fell over the side!" I cries, spitting.

I shows Dad the goose egg at the back of my head. Himmelman's there, he reaches down to touch it and he comes up with blood.

"By God!" he roars. "There'll be no more of this!"

He goes down to get the men up. Once he's got them standing together on the deck he lights into them. "I never seen such a miserable pack of men would do this to a boy!" he's shouting. "By God, that's the end of it. Anything more like this and I'll take the vessel into Lunenburg and dump the bunch of you and get myself a new crew. And it wouldn't surprise me if I did a lot better with them. What kind of men are you? Murderers? Are you a bunch of filthy murderers? I tell you, if I gets ahold of the man who knocked this boy over the side I'll break his neck. Don't think I won't do it. I'll bait the trawls with him. Do you hear what I'm saying?"

That night took Cathy out of my head. Dad wouldn't let me go about the vessel unless one of my bothers was with me. But the crew stayed out of my way, even Redwis, and there weren't much talk about this Jonah thing.

There weren't no fish either. A week before the trip's up, we got thirty quintals in the hold, just over three thousand pounds in a vessel that can take two hundred times that. I could see Dad was wondering how we'd get by the winter if the summer fishing was no better for us. The day before we heads back Himmelman calls me to his cabin. I comes in and there's Redwis sitting, greasy and bristly, smoking a cigarette.

"Yes, Captain?" I asks Himmelman.

Himmelman's behind his table and he says, "I just want to hear it from you, boy, so we can put this whole thing to rest before we gets to Lunenburg. Redwis won't leave off. He swears that you got no use for God, that you been cursing him up and down."

I stood there, and I looked over at Redwis, and he kept staring straight ahead like when he was telling me his stories about the war. Right then, I made up my mind to say it.

"Captain," I asks, "did Redwis ever tell you what happened to him during the war?"

"I never heard him mention it," says Himmelman, "except about him being a corpsman."

"Well, he told me a lot about it."

"That's so, is it?" Himmelman asks Redwis. Redwis nods and plays with his cigarette, and I go right into her.

"His ambulance got blown apart," I says, "but Redwis survived. He told me it was then he felt God was out to get him. When he come home from the war he found everyone that had gone over had been killed but for one, and that man drowned a few years ago. He said to me, 'Cale, I believe God's at me because I said it made no difference to me he was out there or not. I turned my back on him. Now he's coming after me and he don't care who he has to kill to get at me. It weren't nothing to him to blow up that ambulance or wipe out the men of my town. I expect he'll kill everyone on the *Heather B Sarty* if he has to, just to get his hands on me.'"

Redwis done the best I could have hoped he'd do. He come off his chair and throwed himself on me and started choking the daylights out of me. "You bastard!" he's screaming. "You little bastard!" Himmelman tried to pull him off but he couldn't get him loose, so he grabbed the chair and brought it down on Redwis' back. Redwis is lying there groaning and Himmelman's standing over him and saying, "You're finished here, Redwis. When we gets in you're gone. I'll not have the likes of you fishing off of my vessel."

That was it for Redwis Cross. But it was God I was fighting, not Redwis. God wanted at my family and he didn't want Cale Fitch getting in his way, so he had Redwis come at me in the dark and pitch me overboard. If we'd of been under sail, that would of been it, they'd never have got to me in time. That's the kind of dirt God likes playing with. When I come out at Redwis it was really God I was coming out at, and I had to play her hard. That's the only way you can fight him. Go at him as tough as he goes at you.

Joshua come and sat down on my bunk when he heard what Redwis had done. "How's your throat, boy?" he asks me.

"I'm all right," I says. "Just the red marks."

"They'll bruise." I seen him shift his body to get more comfortable and his shoulders strained against his flannel shirt. His face had gone right serious. "Look, boy. Jonathan Daniel's off in his dreamworld these days and I don't think either of the twins could help you out much in a jam. But if there's any kind of trouble next trip, you stick close to me. Nobody'll lay a hand on you, so help me."

Looking at Joshua, just turned twenty-one, you'd swear you saw the old man in the set of his jaw. I had to smile, thinking of the way he used to imitate Jonathan Daniel. Dad counted on Joshua a lot more than he did Jonathan Daniel now. Joshua knew it and he'd taken on the role expected of him. You could see he was comfortable with it and had come into his own.

"Thank you," I tells him. "I'd feel good about that."

He gives me a light punch on the shoulder and heads back on deck. It was the first time I thought of Joshua as an older brother.

Redwis was standing on the dock when we was getting ready to cast off for the summer trip. "Watch her," he keeps saying to our new men, maybe five or six of them. "She's got a Jonah on board. Oh yes. You go ahead and ask how much fish they's brought in this year."

Finally, it's Himmelman comes down to him. "I guess it's time to go, Mister Cross," he says.

"There ain't no law against me standing here."

So help me, that Himmelman was just a little bit of a man, but he puts them shrivelled eyes of his on Redwis and he says, "I'll break your bloody neck, Redwis."

Redwis takes a good look at him, as if he might start something, then he snorts and walks away, pushing his hair back. We heard he got on with the *Sadie Mosher.* You could say we'd been something of friends once. But he'd tried to kill me and you don't get cozy with the man tries to do you in. I spoke with Redwis only one more time.

The first day back on the Banks you'd think our luck had changed. It was good fishing. We put thirty quintals in the hold, as much as we'd hauled up in two months of spring fishing. Supper was like a party. The cook roasted up some salt beef and made a huge cake full of frosting. There was all kinds of singing, you'd of thought it was Sunday. We went to bed dreaming of a trip that would fill our pockets and make up for the hard times of the spring.

You got to understand this about the fisherman on the Banks. The business is lean from first to last. You're away from home seven to eight months of the year and your family's got to live on whatever money you've left behind. If you don't come back in ahead it makes things that much worse. We always done all right because there were six of us working. But the man that's got no sons, what's he going to do? The fish don't bite, he's the one has to make up for it on the other end. There's the fog and the slop ice and the wind. There's the rowing. There's the hooks coming up looking for your fingers or your face. There's the storms. The dory's the best boat a man can make but they ain't fish and they don't swim. How about the rain dropping down on you? It gets under your oils and you're wet the rest of the trip. Nothing ever dries. Your hands crack open and your fingers get like wood. When the fishing's done there's the catch to dress down. What if you ain't watching, or you're tired, and the knife goes into your hand? You can't go out in the dories, you don't get a fair share when you tie up at Lunenburg. If we could of broke free of the sea most of us would of been making our living someplace else.

It's why the men starts getting desperate when the next week goes by and the catch gets less and less. Himmelman moves us from bank to bank but we haul the hooks up empty. He's got me and Dad praying out loud with the crew every Sunday, but even the weather don't

go our way. There was one time we couldn't put the dories over for
five days in a row, that's how bad the seas were. Everybody starts
remembering Redwis and his talk, and one of the new men says to
me one morning, "You dirty little bugger. Get off of our vessel."

I doesn't say nothing to him, but I seen some of the men glancing
at me over their coffee and mugs of tea. Dad's talking one day out in
the boat, "The men are getting superstitious again. I never seen
such a vessel for it. You stick close to me or Joshua. It'll come to a
head pretty soon if the fishing don't pick up. How's it going for you,
Cale?"

"I don't know."

"You remember the verse your mother put on your cake?"

"Yes."

"You hold onto that. It'll see you through."

He smiles and starts singing a song, not a hymn, but a song about
the beauty of the sea, how she watches over the man who respects
her and spends his life learning her moods. I found it good to look at
the shine of her back, the slow turn of her shoulder. But when the
dories come back in it's only a couple of quintals that are laid head to
tail between the layers of salt and you can feel the crew shifting in its
sleep in the dark.

The next day was Sunday. We sang a few hymns and Dad gave a
bit of a message about Peter and the big catch of fish, how Peter
didn't believe God could do it. I seen the men weren't listening. The
sky was blank. It felt like we were baking in some kind of tin hut.

After lunch most of the crew was napping on deck, a few like
Aaron just staring out at the water. Matthew was off by himself splic-
ing some rope. Jonathan Daniel was straddling the bowsprit, sketch-
ing. Joshua was lying down next to me. I was making a show of reading my Bible. The cable grunted as the vessel spun slowly around it,
like the hand of a clock.

It was Seraphim Levy spoke up. "I tell you, young Fitch," he says
to me in a voice like old wood splintering, "your grandad done the
same thing with his Bible, going over it every Sunday for all the
world to see, and I don't know as it done him any good at the end of
it all. The Almighty knowed the heart of him and he drowned him
for us so the *Angela Price* could make it in safe. I guess the two of
you was cut out of the same length of wood."

I looked over at Seraphim. He was one of the new men and he was huge, something a cooper might of put together, belly as round and hard as a hoop of staves. He was all over him hair, it come out of his ears, it come out his nose, it was all around his eyes, his beard covered the whole of his throat. To see him propped up somewhere you thought of a rock setting in the middle of a forest trailing some of that long white moss. I don't say he was pretty. His face was hasty. Flesh and bone didn't come together. One eye was higher than the other. The cheeks had the eyes almost squeezed shut.

Dad was nearby working at the carving of a gull with his knife. He doesn't even look up but asks, "What is it you're saying, Seraph?"

Seraphim sits up against the main mast, his shirt open and hair sprouting like a ditch of weeds. He pays no attention to Dad and starts talking to the whole crew. "It was just the same," he's saying. "The *Angela Price* done so poorly on the Banks that year the Captain asked us did we want to take on a winter run to the West Indies. We all decided to go. Took a load of lumber and a bit of fish. It was fine heading out. I thought I knowed all about Isaac Fitch then. A father, a fishing man, a farmer, a good Christian. Bible in his lap every Sunday afternoon, just like his grandson there. We come to Jamaica and he's drunk and raising hell every night. You never seen Isaac for days at a time. One of the boys told me they seen him go on like this when they tied up at Boston a few years before. It was like you get him far enough away from Cape Race and he goes at her like the Devil."

I glanced over at Dad while this was going on. He never bothered to look at Seraphim once during the whole story, just stuck to his carving, shaping the gull's beak with short, sharp cuts.

"We got our load of rum and salt," Seraphim keeps on, "and after near a month we headed on back. First Sunday, out come the Bible. You wanted to spit. But no one said a thing. He had a temper that man, and he'd go at you with a knife before he'd use his fists.

"It's not a week out and the swells start rising. This mess of cloud comes out of the south and rain, you couldn't get a breath was you on deck. We had everything in but the jumbo and still I thought we was going to put our bow under and go straight down. You couldn't eat, even could you keep it down the vessel was jogging so sharp the cook couldn't get a hot meal to your mouth. Two days of this and the wind is at us both fists. The watch come running down. 'It's a water spout,' he yells. 'The Captain wants every one of you on deck.'

"We gets in our oils and climbs out, and there, this snake of black water heading for us across the sea. It was fearful. The Captains says, 'We start busting up, cut the boats loose. If some of you come out of it, there's chance of a clipper picking you up.'

"That thing come on and on, and then hung back, like it was trying to make up its mind to break us up or not. We was all in a bunch at the stern of the vessel, but it's Isaac who starts walking toward the bow. There's great blasts of wind hitting the boat, and you seen the foremast break away just then, come right over like a cut tree. It caught Isaac across the back, crushed the life out of him. The Captain run to get at him, but the mast rolled right into the sea and it dragged Isaac with it. He got tossed up once and then the waves hauled him under. It was a terrible thing to watch, and look, from the mast falling to Isaac going under is maybe half a minute. You hardly had time to think what was happening. We was watching that water spout and it hung there for a couple more minutes, then it cut across our wake and headed for land. The wind dropped, and the rain slacked off some, and soon the Captain run up the mainsail.

"There was talk about all of this, but it was easy enough to see what had gone on. God sent a water spout for Isaac and he didn't want to kill all of us to get at him. So the wind waited on Isaac to move, and when he did, she brought that mast on him as clean as I ever seen a pine dropped. We had no more trouble getting in and that spring it seemed like there was fish on every hook. God had his way with Isaac, he'll have his way with the grandson. You watch and see if he don't. I just hope he gets at it soon. I got to earn some money this trip if I want to get Nilda and me through the winter."

When he'd done, all of it was sitting on us, the heat, Isaac, the empty hold, me with the Bible open in my lap. Even Dad don't say a thing until one of the men gets up and growls, "Let's drop the bugger off at an outport and be done with him."

Dad stands, placing his carving carefully on the deck. "You don't touch the boy," he says. "He's a good fisherman and he stays with the vessel."

But it's another man tells Dad, "We ain't got five boys bringing money in to feed our families, Fitch. We'll put him off tomorrow."

"No," says Dad. "I guess not."

"The hell with you," snarls the man. "You don't run the vessel. Who's for putting the boy off?"

There was enough voices for it, I tell you. Joshua got up and stood over me while Jonathan Daniel crawled down off the bowsprit. Matthew and Aaron walked through the crowd of men to stand beside Dad. Seraphim says, "I guess we got something to tell the Captain."

Himmelman's coming up on deck and he asks, "What's that, Seraph?"

"We want young Fitch off the *Heather B,* old man. We want him dropped at an outport."

"Is that what you been on about, Seraph? Took a vote on it and everything, did you?"

"Yes."

"I don't give a damn for your vote. This is my vessel. I decide who stays with me. The boy's a good worker. I'd put most of you off before I would him."

"I guess we know how to handle a schooner," Seraph tells Himmelman, and he pushes himself to his feet. "Haul up that cable," he orders the crew.

Three or four of the men start for the bow and a couple more go to put up the foresail. Himmelman brings this old black revolver from the back of his belt and holds it so everyone can get a look.

"By God," he says, "I'll shoot the first man so much as touches a rope."

Seraphim says, "He won't do it. Let's get that cable up."

Himmelman walks over to Seraphim and just like that he smacks the revolver into the side of his head. Seraphim ducks and tries to get ahold of the gun, but Himmelman hits Seraphim's hands with it and that gets him hollering. Himmelman gives him another crack on the side of the head and this time Seraphim goes down. There's Himmelman dangling the barrel of the revolver over Seraphim's head, saying, "If any of you tries to lift that cable I'll get Seraph with the first shot and you with the second."

There's no one moving but Seraphim, rocking back and forth on the deck.

"All of you get down below," Himmelman orders the crew. "Mister Fitch and his boys stay here."

The men start down and one of them goes over to help Seraphim, but Himmelman waves him off. "He stays with me."

When they's all below Himmelman locks them in and turns to me. "Come midnight,"he says, "when the Sabbath's over, we'll make for Sable Island. If the weather stays good, we'll go in there and get us some fish. You think you and your brothers can sail this vessel?"

"Yes," I tells him.

And that's what it come to. At twelve, it was six of us and Seraphim that hauled up the cable and hoisted the sails. It was a warm night, but a bit of wind had come up out of the north-east and it took us along right nice. The sky was thick with stars, I suppose Jonathan Daniel would of called it a night of fire. Himmelman himself takes the wheel and when we're on our way he calls me over.

"How about you have a go at the wheel?" he says.

"I never tried it."

"Go ahead," he says and steps aside.

So I takes ahold of that helm and it's like you're driving a team of good horses. We had a full press of canvas up, and going straight down that night everything was white and dark to me, it's like there was nothing else.

"She's doing eleven knots," Himmelman tells me, "maybe twelve now and then. She's quick. There ain't no fish to weigh us down."

It was like the stars was part wind and streaming by us. I seen Dad and my brothers up by the bow, and Seraphim was back to sitting against the mast, but it wasn't like they was with me. The *Heather B* would heel and I'd go with her, she'd cut deep into that water and I could feel her. Even Himmelman wasn't there. He'd say something and it's like a part of the boat was speaking.

"I had her built before the war," comes this voice. "I wanted a vessel that could go with the wind. You see, I been on a few clippers when I was your age. Went all the way to China, boy. Some times they were. We'd race another clipper did we see one. I wanted that. Clouds and big seas, winds that come on at you. So I made up my mind to be a captain. Had the *Heather B* built in Lunenburg and I drew up the plans myself. I knowed what it had to be.

"She's moving tonight. Does you ever get a vessel, Cale, make sure the wind is built into her. Some of the boats they're building now, they think all that matters is making a living. Plenty of room for the fish, but they're slow and heavy. And then they're putting in steam. Why, there's no life to those vessels. They're dead before they put them in the water. A fishing man doesn't have a night like this here in his lifetime, I don't know why he bothers to go out on the sea. If making a living is all he wants, he might as well move to Halifax and get a desk and a window. It ain't just making a living."

Himmelman's hand comes down over mine and moves the wheel a couple of inches to the right.

"There," he says, "keep her fine. We'll be at Sable by sunrise. You'll take her right in."

I did that too. The sun come on behind us, but the colour of it run right over the sea like somebody had slit a bag of grain. Sable was a long white beach, someplace you'd want to stay and put your feet in the water. That's how she looked when the weather was fine. Give her a good wind and she was the Devil. It was Seraphim took the soundings, the first time I heard him speak.

"Forty fathom," he calls out.

"Take everything in but the jumbo," orders Himmelman, and Dad and my brothers go to it.

"Thirty-five fathom," calls Seraphim. "Now it's forty again ...forty-eight...fifty-two..."

"It's the sand," Himmelman tells me. "Always moving from one place to the other. She'll come off to thirty again in a couple of minutes."

"Thirty-two!" shouts Seraphim all of a sudden. "Thirty! Twenty-seven!"

"Get ready to drop anchor," cries Himmelman.

"Twenty-five fathom!" Seraphim is calling back from the bow. "Twenty-three! Twenty!"

"Let her go!" shouts Himmelman. "Aaron and Matthew, bring in the jumbo!"

Twenty fathoms off of Sable, that ain't much water between you and the island. A good swell come up and you're onto her in five minutes. But Himmelman was risking it. He knowed there'd be cod in there that close, feeding off the sand.

Seraphim come back from the bow as the *Heather B Sarty* hung steady at the end of her cable.

"Eighteen fathom," he says.

Himmelman goes over and unlocks the door and calls down to the crew, "Let's bait her up."

The men went at it with a hard look to them, but they done it. Just over an hour and we was in our oils, on deck, and ready to dump the dories over the side. Some of the men starts muttering when they sees how close we's tucked into Sable. Himmelman didn't pay any attention, just waited for the last couple of men to get squared away. Then he faced us as we stood by our dories.

"It's the boy brought us in here from the Banks,"he says. "His hand on the wheel. And it's him and his Dad going to be the first dory out. We'll wait on them. When we see they've got fish, every one of you will go out and set your trawl. We'll fill the hold before we leave this place."

He jerks his head at me and Dad and we go over. I pays out our trawl as we sail down towards Sable, and by the time it's set an hour later we was so close to the north-west arm I could of throwed a rock onto it.

"Dad," I asks as I'm furling the small canvas sail, "all that Seraph said about Grandad Isaac, was he talking a straight line?"

"I don't know," Dad answers. "I never saw a lot of my father. But I was at the back end of his temper a few times. I don't like to say it, but he could of gone that way. I'll tell you this though. He meant it when he read that Bible of his. He's got notes scribbled all through it. I think he come to it looking for mercy."

I turns and looks back at the vessel. "What's Himmelman going to do we don't get a bite?"

"Boy, I don't believe the old man's thought on that. We're in close to Sable, the weather's good, and he knows you got a faith in God."

"All right."

"It's going to be taken care of, Cale. It's got to be. We'll let the trawl go another ten minutes and I'm going to pray on it."

Dad bows his head and hunches over in the stern, his big hands wound together and his thumbs almost touching his forehead. When he prayed it was like he was talking another language, all full of thee's and thou's. But there weren't nothing said for show. He went at it hard. When he was done he lifts his head and says, "Let's haul her up, Cale. The boys are waiting on us." Then he reaches down. "Get ahold of your gaff," he tells me.

We starts under-running the trawl and I'm bringing the hooks in over the roller and there's nothing. Five, ten minutes, the hooks empty, we're working our way back to the vessel. I think I can see some of the men moving around to get a better look at us, but it can't be, we're still over a mile away, and I'm taking all these cuts on my hands as I'm pulling in the trawl with my stick.

"Easy, boy," Dad warns.

It's half a mile and there's still nothing, and I'm sure the men can see us now, can see there's no catch for us here either. I'm hauling, jerking the line out of the water, hands cold, the sun burning in the sea.

The first cod come. It was a big fish. I gaffed her off and there was another slapping over the roller. You couldn't sit back and think on it. Cod was coming in every fifteenth hook, every seventy-five feet of line. I'm knocking them into the bottom of the boat and Dad's baiting up as the hooks run by him. We're to our shins in fish in maybe half an hour and still they's coming in. I starts laughing and Dad's hollering and the water's breaking bright with fish, and the next thing I hears is the dories going over the side.

Joshua tells us later, "The old man's waiting for a signal from one of you and then he sees you're bent over working the trawl so hard. 'In the name of God,' he yells, 'get the dories over the side!" And that's what we done, the bunch of us running and shouting and pulling at the boats. The way we went at it, why, you'd of thought there's none of us had ever seen cod on a hook before!"

All day we was out there and half of the night. You seen the torches stuck onto the trawl tubs and these flames are moving back and forth with the dories like candles in a dark house. My hands are bright one moment, black the next, jerking in and out of the light with the gaff, and the fish are falling past my boots white. The wood of the oars is thumping across the water, the fish are kicking as we haul up, the hooks are snapping against the roller, and back of it all is the slashed breath of struggling men. Every time we trawls back to the *Heather B* we got fish to unload and the cook's there to pry coffee and biscuits between cold fingers. It was past midnight before Himmelman blows the whistle. We hoisted all ten of the dories on board and headed for our bunks. It was two hours sleep we got that first night and then back over the sides to set our trawls.

That next day was clear and warm, and it's like the fish was jumping out of the water at us when we hauled up the hooks. We come in for a bit of lunch after two sets, and there's the little boys of the dress gang full of blood and going at it and no break for them. It was something. There was no stopping again that night. Dawn come like a sharp cut and we're still there hauling up. We had a mug-up about eight but that's all Himmelman done for us. At nine, we're in the dories again and heading down for our marker buoys. I kept expecting to haul up an empty trawl and there's an end to it, but no, the cod was dropping over the side thick as before. The sun's hot, you're sweating inside of your oils, but your hands are cold. There's the pain tearing up your back, and your face, it's like someone's working lines into it with a knife.

We was at it four days and three nights without any kind of real sleep, but when the fish run like that, it's what you do. Seraphim Levy fainted over his trawl line, and Matthew almost fell off of the vessel after we'd pulled up the dories to get ourselves a bite to eat. It come to the fourth night and we was all rowing and hauling and gaffing like old men. You could hardly remember the name of the vessel you was fishing off of or the name of the man you was working with. It's evening and the sun gone, and I'm hauling at the line, and I slips, and that's it, I can't get to my feet, I'm just looking up at Dad's face like it's the head of another cod.

"Ain't you a big bugger?" I says. "I'd need a proper gaff for you."

"I guess you would," Dad answers, and he stands over me and brings the rest of the line in himself, the fish dropping onto my back and head and all around me.

"I could start cleaning them in the boat," I tells him. "That would save us some work on the vessel."

"No," Dad says. "I expect the whistle will come along in another ten minutes or so."

It come in less that that. What a chore hauling all them dories onto the deck. Some men was pulling, and some was falling down, and some was just standing there watching it all. The dress gang needed a hand, so I picked up a knife and went back to my old job of taking the heads off. That's a couple of hours and then I'm sitting at one of the tables down below staring at this mess of salt cod on my plate.

"Go ahead," Dad coaxes me. "It's hot."

But I never lifted my fork. I just sat there looking at this plate of salt cod. Joshua said it's like I was waiting for it to do something. When it come time to head for the bunks, it's Dad had to pick me up. I guess I slept some. It's the morning was the worst. They wake us up and it's like my stomach is full of a lot of prickly hemp wound tight.

"I can't," I tells Dad. "I'm going to be sick."

"A few more days of this and that'll be the end of it," he promises me. "The old man says the hold is pretty near full up already."

So I'm out there laying down the trawl line again. It's two more days of it, and just as many nights, and Himmelman giving us about two hours of sleep every morning. I tell you, I was somewhere else them days, I sure weren't with Dad in the boat.

Jonathan Daniel come out of the light of the sun one afternoon and he says, "This is all right for me, Cale. I gets a lot of strength from the fire."

"That's not a good place to be," I tells him, squinting at his face and trailing my fingers in the water. "You seen what happened to them hogs."

"It's a different fire," Jonathan Daniel says, sitting down in front of me. "It works on your soul, breaks it down. You get small enough for God."

"What happens to you?"

"You don't see these things anymore. You leave the sea and the fish and the boats."

"Where do you go?"

"To God. You see what I'm saying?"

"I'm not sure."

"God is fire. You got to be fire to get close to him. The fire's working on you, Cale, trying to make you a part of it. But you won't let it take you."

"I like it right here. I'm just a bit tired."

"I guess you are, Cale. It takes a lot out of you to hold back that fire.

And he shows me this sketch of the men fishing in the dark, and it's flames they're hauling into their dories, there's flames under the sea and flames burning in the sky over the boats, and five or six men are bursting with fire, but the other men are so dark you can hardly see them.

"There you are," Jonathan Daniel says.

He puts a finger on a boy in one of the boats, and you can only see him because of the man next to him, all bright and full of light.

It come out that we filled the hold and Himmelman swore it was because of me. A lot of the crew believed him too, they come to me to say they was sorry for what happened that Sunday. Even Seraphim come by. It's an afternoon when we're celebrating the catch and Aaron's upcoming marriage at the same time, and it's a mug of rum Seraphim brings with him when he puts himself beside me and Dad.

"I'll tell you what it is," he says to the two of us. "I was raised pretty strict. I was made to know what was right and what was wrong, what was the work of the Devil and what was the work of the Lord. It was cut and dried. I got a thrashing once for bringing home a deck of cards. I didn't even know what they was. I found them near a pile of trash. I thought the coloured cards was some nice. So I put them in my pocket. You'd of thought I'd gone to hell itself to find them the way my mother went on. I come to believe in the Devil a lot more than I come to believe in God.

"I weren't supposed to go to dances either. But the minister's son would stand outside of the hall where the dance was going on and he'd pick fights. Nobody said nothing about that. I'm standing out there with him one time and he starts whaling away on the Slauenwhite boy. I couldn't take it, so I went into the hall to get away from the two of them. The next day my Dad gets ahold of me and throws me across the kitchen, starts going at me with his fists. The minister's son had come by to tell him I gone into the dance hall the night before. That's how it was. I was taught there was some things a Christian didn't do and the worst of them was drinking and dancing and gambling and swearing. Did you go at these things God would lay into you sooner or later.

"My brother Len was going out with some of the boys into the bush and drinking and none of us knowed about it. I'm with him in the ox cart one day and the whole thing goes over into a ditch, rolls right over the top of us. A couple of inches this way or that we would of been crushed. It come out a week later about the boys drinking down in the woods and Dad takes the strap to Len. He says to him, 'Here you could of got your brother killed and he didn't do a thing wrong. Was just you playing your game with the Devil.'

"It's all of this sticks in my head. So when I seen Isaac holding a Bible one day and a bottle the next, what do you think? The way I sees it, he's a Christian doing wrong and God's going to go after him, the same as he gone after Len that day on the ox cart. I was sure the Lord was going to drown the whole of us on the *Angela Price* just to get at Isaac.

"Now, I hears all about the boy being the Jonah the day I put my gear on the *Heather B Sarty*, and I make up my mind to wait and see if it's so. Why, it was like going out to sea in the *Angela Price* again. You seen yourself how we had no fish to speak of. The only thing I could think of was God was coming after the boy to settle up with him, and did I want to see Nilda again I had to get Cale off the boat. I see I was wrong about him. Something of God's going right along with you, boy. I never seen such fishing as we had this past week. He's doing good to you and here we gets ahold of some of it at the same time.

"But I tell you, there's still someone behind all of that poor fishing. I'm sure of that. It's just that God's for the young Cale here more than he's against this other fellow. I hope it stays that way. I only got a few more years of the work left in me and I need the vessels filled for every one of them. You do what you can for me, will you, boy?"

"All right," I says to him and it's a nod he gives me before he leaves the table.

We come into Lunenburg and I'm feeling good, I'm thinking I took on God and won. Aaron was in high spirits, laughing at the ribbing the crew was giving him, sitting near the bow with his thin arms crossed over his knees, his red and blue flannel shirt puffed in the wind, his green eyes throwing out light. Him and Dad headed into Bridgewater to see Cathy and her family, and Himmelman put me and my brothers up for a few days.

He had a bright yellow house high on the hill across from the graveyard. It was a big place, full of small wooden ships and sea paintings he'd pulled out of magazines and framed. Every table had something on it, and the chairs and sofas were hidden behind stacks of books and photograph albums. Himmelman didn't have no kids and he didn't have no wife, but once a week a woman come to do whatever cleaning he allowed her to do.

He put the four of us in one double bed and said it was up to us to get our own meals. I could hardly sleep. Joshua's grinding his teeth, Matthew's turning from one side to the other, and I'm lying there next to Jonathan Daniel and he's cold as ice. It was three or four days we was supposed to sleep like that, but I made up my mind after the first night I was going to get ahold of a quilt and lie on the floor. I never got around to it. Aaron and Dad was back the next afternoon.

Aaron wouldn't talk to any of us. He goes on ahead to get our dinghy ready for sailing and Dad tells us, "There'll be no wedding. Cathy's changed her mind."

We get back to Tarragon and Aaron takes over every chore there is, hauling water from the well, chopping wood, making repairs around the house. You try and give him a hand with some of it and he pretty near tears your head off. So we let him alone. He'd take one of the boats and row out by himself and spend the day on the water. Mom would be looking out her window and fretting.

"I should of known," she'd say. "I shouldn't of let him spend all that time with that girl and her family."

"Nothing wrong with the girl or her family," Dad would tell her. "People got a right to change their minds."

"I guess it's her mother put her up to it," Mom would keep on, stretching her neck to get a sight of Aaron in the boat. "I don't believe she wanted her girl marrying a fisherman."

"That Cathy had a mind of her own," Dad would say. "If she wanted to marry Aaron her mother wouldn't of been able to stop her."

"He's well rid of her then," Mom would decide. "It's her that's on the losing end, not Aaron. A good boy like him will have no trouble finding the right girl a few years down the road."

It come on to Christmas and Aaron's getting back like himself, talking a bit, smiling down at the table when he feels good about something, even spending time with Matthew. He never gone out and shot sea duck before, but he done that now, and he'd bring them in for Mom to cook up. It's like another part of him was growing out.

"The whole thing's doing him good," Dad says. "He's learning to handle himself instead of taking a swing at someone."

A snow come down one night and the island was white when we got up in the morning. Aaron rows out in the boat, and I start walking up to the lighthouse, putting my footprints next to Charlie Zinck's, the keeper. The rifle goes off, sounding strong and clean in all that white, and I takes a look to see if Aaron's been lucky, but there was this bit of a fog down, I couldn't see the boat. I spent the morning talking with Charlie. Charlie loved to talk as long as the conversation run in deep waters. At noon, I headed down to the house for lunch.

"You seen your brother?" Mom asks me as I come in the door.

"Which one?" I asks. "Aaron?"

"I can't see him. It could be he's got himself lost in that fog."

"Oh, I don't think. He's been out in a lot worse than this."

Dad and Matthew come up from the fish store just as Joshua and Jonathan Daniel come downstairs. Mom asks, "Father, will you go after Aaron for me?"

"You're fretting too much," he tells her, taking his cap off and sitting down at the table. "He'll be in when he's hungry. How about some tea for us?"

We had our lunch and Dad heads back to the store with Matthew and Joshua. Me and Jonathan Daniel is chopping up wood when Mom comes out hugging her sweater around her.

"Will you boys go looking for your brother for me?" she asks. "I can't see him yet and there ain't been any shooting since this morning."

"All right, Mom," says Jonathan Daniel. "Cale and I will go out and bring him in."

We went and put the other dory in the water and we rows out to the south of the island. I brought a conch along and I'd keep blowing into it as we're going through all of the mist. But Aaron never called back to us and we never seen the boat.

"He might of drifted," says Jonathan Daniel, so we headed east of the island, shouting his name. We was at it two or three hours, but we never come onto him.

"He'll catch it when he gets in," Jonathan Daniel says. "We might as well head back."

We'd just pulled the dory up and was walking to the house when Charlie Zinck come running down to us through the snow in his shirt sleeves.

"Listen," he says, "I seen your brother's boat through a break in the fog. He's north of the island and just drifting. You want to head that way and help him out."

We ran for Dad and he got the bunch of us into the dinghy and we sailed her right around the island. The fog was coming off some so we seen the boat and come down to her, but Aaron never answered any of our shouts. Dad brought in the sail and we paddled the dinghy right up to the dory before we saw him.

He's lying flat in the bottom of the boat, and the rifle's in his lap pointing up at his head, and his head's gone. Matthew puts his hands over his face and starts yelling, "I don't want to see it, I don't want to see it." Dad gets Jonathan Daniel to hold the two boats together so's he can step down into the dory. "Oh, my God," I hears Joshua say. "Aaron." Dad lifts Aaron and gives him to Joshua and me until he can climb back on board. Then he takes him and lays him in the stern and wraps a grey blanket around his body.

It's Joshua ties the dory on behind and Jonathan Daniel puts up our sail. Dad sits next to Aaron, and he puts one hand on Aaron's shoulder and the other on the tiller, and that's how we comes back in. Dad carries him up from the landing and the snow's falling again, soft and thick, and we leaves our footprints on the path as we walks up to the house. You would of thought it would be pretty in some kind of sad way, the dark coming on, the snow falling gold through the lamp light of the porch, candles burning in a couple of the windows, the sharp smell of the woodsmoke, the four of us trailing behind Dad who's stepping tall and steady up to the door, but no, there weren't no beauty to it, the island was pale and full of cold.

We buried him near the woods on the west end of Tarragon. Hank come in for that. He asked me did I want to make a prayer or read something out of the Bible, but I told him no. Dad took me aside when we was dressing in our blue serge suits on the Friday morning and he says, "It would mean a lot to your mother and me was you to help Hank with the service."

It weren't in me to take the game that far. I gives Dad this look and I says right out, "No. I want nothing to do with God or praying.

He's taking our family piece by piece and you're too blind to see it."

Dad stops knotting his tie in the mirror and drops his hands to his side, as if he's waiting to take a blow but not hit back. He keeps looking into the mirror. "What are you saying, Cale?"

"I'm through with the Bible reading and praying and all this about me being a minister. I'd soonef go to hell than spend my life serving the kind of God you're running after. You can take me off of the *Heather B Sarty* if you want. I'm done with the whole farce."

"That's what it's been to you all this time, boy? A farce? An act?"

"Dad, I'm trying to save this family, I'm trying to keep you out of God's hands. Don't you see what he is?"

"You never gave yourself to God, did you? The baptism, your praying with the crew, your Bible in your lap. You never meant a bit of it."

"How else could I of stayed on the Banks? I had to play the game or you wouldn't of let me go out with you. I can't protect you if I ain't close to you, I can't keep you from drowning."

But Dad had turned and was walking quickly down the stairs. I felt like I'd been watching the two of us from a distance. It took a lot to make my body move, to get myself to the staircase.

"I promised Mom!" I yelled at his back, but he kept going and I heard a door open and close.

My suit was tight. The whole time at the cemetery a wind was going right through me. Joshua was standing stiff and firm next to Mom and had an arm around her. Dad was dark and steady on her other side. Mom didn't move, her eyes were grey and focused past all of us. It was like she were a large cliff and the waves beating against her. Matthew stood by himself, back of the group around the grave. His face was round and white, and under his eyes dark red welts glimmered, as if he'd been struck. Jonathan Daniel you couldn't hardly see, he mingled in with the other people, though every now and then I seen him thin and black and swaying a bit in the gusts of wind.

Angus Young was standing near me and I felt so cold and terrible I wanted to take it out on him. I didn't believe he gave a damn for Aaron, I guessed he was there because he had to be, the island was so small. Hank talked too long, I think, too long for me. I wanted to get away from the mud and the cold and Aaron. When we come back to the house, and the people was eating bits of cake and drinking coffee, I felt like knocking the table over and spilling the coffee and food in their laps. We're all sitting there in our church clothes, and talking quiet, and moving right slow and careful, it was like we was acting something out.

When everybody had left I showed Mom how bad my suit fit me and she said we'd have to see about getting another one. I tears that thing off my back, and I puts it in a bag, and I heads up to the grave with it. The men was going to come back later and fill it in, but I threw my suit on top of Aaron and took one of the shovels and did the job myself. Then I went over to the cliffs and watched the wind fighting back and forth with the sea.

Dad took me down to the fish store that night, and we lights a lantern, and we sits there facing each other.

"I can't help it," I says. "Damn God for what he's doing to our family."

Dad spoke right quiet. "It weren't God took down the rifle."

"If Aaron hadn't gone to that church social he wouldn't of met her."

"Look, boy, it's hard for me to find good in any of this. But I don't see how it's got to be God we blame for it. That's the way you used to talk, laying every piece of bad luck to him, and now you're at it again. It's a pity you didn't spend less time pretending to be a Christian and more time with your brother Aaron. You might of been good friends."

I couldn't keep my eyes on Dad's, so I just crossed my arms over my chest and looked down at a tin of paint brushes soaking in turpentine. After a bit, Dad got up.

"I ain't going to keep you back from the fishing, Cale," he says to me. "I still want the two of us hauling trawl together. But I'm telling you, boy, you're going to hurt a lot of the people around you with this notion of yours. We thought you'd growed out of it and here you're chewing at it yet. Getting to be there ain't nothing else to you but that."

He walked out of the store and I sat there with the lantern another half-hour before I come up to the house. Mom was in the kitchen and she asks me, "Where's your father?"

"I don't know," I tells her. "He went up ahead of me."

"I ain't seen him," she says, taking a can of flour out of a cupboard over her head.

"Well, I seen him and he walked out of the store ahead of me."

Mom turns on me, her hands resting on the top of the counter. "You're not talking that way to me, Cale Fitch!" she's almost shouting. "Your brother would be alive tonight but for you. Going around behind our backs and turning people against God, and all the time telling everyone you was going to be a minister. Why, you don't care who you lie to so long as you get what you want. Come eighteen, I want you out of this house. I don't care how you make a living, but you're not staying under the same roof with us. You knowed someone in the family might of got hurt was you to keep on with your talk, making God out to be the Devil. But you never let up. Any of your brothers could of been drowned on the Banks, but you would of kept right up with it. You could of lost your own Dad. All that matters to you is those foolish ideas of yours. Go on, get out of my sight. I got no use for you. And take them filthy boots off your feet, you're tracking mud through the whole house. Hurry up!"

Mom went at me the whole winter. There was no forgiving what I done. I never got up early enough to suit her. I never chopped enough wood. I never had the stoves hot enough. I didn't help Dad around the place enough. Almost every time I tried to say something to her, she cut me off and said she had no time to listen to a liar. Come Christmas, I got this nice bowl for her out of my fishing money, picking it up in Lunenburg. When we was opening our gifts, she acted like she never seen it and left it there under the tree. She never touched it. When we come to take the tree down it was still there, sitting wrapped up on the floor. I left it for another week and then I took it away and broke it up.

It weren't just me who got it. Mom took it out on everybody. Jonathan Daniel wasn't eating enough, he was too thin. He wasn't doing his share of the work around the house. He was spending too much time daydreaming and drawing foolish pictures. Joshua was getting in everybody's way, couldn't mind his own business, was off on this crazy notion that he was the only man in the family and had to take care of everything. Dad was sitting reading the Bible too much and all the repairs that needed to be done. He was always idling his time away in the fish store.

She even lit into Matthew and that was the worst of it. The rest of us could handle what she said to us. Matthew couldn't. There wasn't no spirit left to him after he seen Aaron lying in the bottom of the dory. He just kept to himself. He'd stay the whole day in the room he'd shared with Aaron if you let him. He started losing weight.

"I never seen the likes of it," Mom's going at Matthew one day over lunch. "A grown man of twenty moping around the house as if there's nothing left to live for. Don't we feed you right? Ain't you got a roof over your head? I'm the one that ought to be going around dragging my feet. I'm the one that's lost a son. But don't I get you your meals on time, ain't I the one washing and ironing your clothes? Look at the way you dress. It's like you had nothing to wear. Oh my, you'd think you was hard done by, Matthew, to take a look at your face. Well, I tell you, this is life, and you better get used to it."

"That's enough," says Dad, and she turns on him.

"Don't tell me what to do," she says. "You couldn't even discipline your own son. Why, you let Cale do anything he wants. When he started asking all them questions you just let him go right on with it. 'He's got a mind of his own,' you says. Didn't matter what he thought of God, all you cared about was him being a loner like yourself. Look at what you got now. He's full of the Devil. It's like he killed Aaron and sent him to hell all by himself. That's the kind of boy you raised."

"Aaron's not in hell, mother," Dad snaps, putting down his soup spoon. "We've got a good God. He don't keep children out of his heaven."

Mom starts crying right hard, and Dad tells us to finish up eating and leave the room. I'm fixing a step on the porch when he comes through the door and stands looking out over the island.

"I don't want any of you talking back to your mother," he says. "It's a hard time for her. She's got it in her head that somebody that kills themselves goes to hell. She don't hate you, Cale. She's disappointed because she sees you're not going to be a minister, and she's angry because you lied to the two of us. But we'll all do some growing through this, and my guess is the day will come when your mother and you is right close again."

We all had our ways of getting out of Mom's sight when our work was done. Dad coaxed Matthew into doing a few hours of handlining every day, and Joshua would find something to do in the store or in the boat house. Joanthan Daniel, he'd walk out to the cliffs. I started dropping in on Charlie Zinck when he was up at the lighthouse. He done a bit of winter fishing, but most of the time he was there, sitting and looking out over the water. He didn't mind me coming by, and it got so's he expected it, he'd have some tea for me and some biscuits. I let Charlie talk, and I'd listen to everything he said, and Charlie thought a lot of that. He got it in his head that I was a good boy and that Mom was acting out of sorts because of the way Aaron had died.

Charlie was in his forties, but he looked younger. His hair was cut short and the skin on his face and hands was always strong and clean. His eyes was wide, it's like everything he looked at was a surprise to him.

"Death now," he says to me one day, "there's something I don't mind thinking about. I wouldn't want to spend all my time on this island, would I? There'll be a lot more freedom after death. A lot more of everything that's good. Here, it's like we're boxed in. I get short of breath if I work too hard. I got to climb this tower if I want to see anything. I can't fly and I can't swim. My thinking is poor. I love looking at the fish feeding near the rocks, but I got to get hooks into them and kill them if I want to eat. You see? But after we're dead, there'll be this new way of going about things. It's my guess there'll be a lot more of this feeling of everything tying together. Flying and walking and swimming, it'll all be part of the same thing. When you sit on a rock there'll be this feeling of knowing everything that rock is stitched into. A bird nesting or a horse moving along by a fence, the both of them will go into making some sense out of the way that rock's lying or the way a wind'll go along the top of the sea. There won't be no more of this feeling of being cut off from things. And there won't be no strangers. It'll all be of one piece. Do you know what I'm saying?"

"It sounds like we'll have to start all over again," I says.

"We will, but it'll be worth it, and it won't be a hard thing. Every-time you learn something new about how this rock ties into the sea, and the sea into a bit of seed growing into a stalk of corn, it'll be like the best of times. No door's going to be closed, boy. I can hardly wait for it all myself. I like keeping the light and I like going out in the dory. But on this side of death, it's like you're half-awake.''

Charlie would walk around the island on a hot day in his oils, on a rainy day like as not in his shirtsleeves, and in a fall of snow he might add a cap to them shirtsleeves and put his hands deeper into his pockets. So the people on Tancook and Tarragon thought he wasn't all there. The truth of it would be, there was more to him than any ten of the rest put together. He just had his ways about him, that's all. He'd stand on the lantern deck and throw bits of cold pancake to the gulls. He was the only man in the Bay took school by correspondence. He had a cello he'd play some nights, and were it fine out, yes, he'd set it down on the deck and he'd go at her. You could hear the sound of it anywhere on the island. It wasn't a sound the people was used to, it's like it was harsh and soft at the same time. There was an evening some of it got out to me on the cliffs and it seemed the swallows was riding down the wind with it. I told Charlie I'd like to learn to play it and he says, "Let's see how the winter goes and maybe I can show you a thing or two on the beast." But the spring come before we'd got around to it.

None of us went on the frozen bait trip that year on account of Mom. I visited Charlie a lot. I remember Easter Sunday, how we sat on a couple of small chairs he kept inside the lantern. We watched the sun chip the sea till it was all of it light. Then Charlie points to a cross he's got hanging just above the glass. It was made out of two pieces of burnt wood.

"Your brother gave that to me the other day," he says.

"Jonathan Daniel?" I asks.

"Yes. He says, 'Happy Easter, Mister Zinck.' I was glad to have it."

"Why?"

"I'll tell you. When I first decided to take on the lighthouse it was important to me that I go about it in the proper frame of mind. I didn't want it to be just a job. You're out there bringing men in through a storm or thick fog or a night. There's something to that. It's the sort of work you still want to have a man doing no matter what kind of world. I guess I seen that's what God done, come out here to get us back through all of this. It's not as if he don't know what it's like on the water. I would say he's had his share of cold and wind. I think of him out there with every boat that's going by the island, hands full of cuts from fish hooks and hauling on the nets. I see us as working together. Every time I climb up here there's two things I do. I has myself some coffee and I has a prayer. I believe God wants the men in off the sea as bad as I does."

"A lot of men die out there. Maybe God ain't the kind of partner you think he is."

"I wouldn't say that. I never knowed him but to die with every one of them."

"The way I see it, God's the one killing them."

"I'll tell you. I'm not saying God don't go hard on a man if there's a reason for it. But I would guess he's for the good of any man goes out in the boats. You says a lot of men die. Well, boy, a lot more of them makes it back in. You take a look at that and you tell me there ain't nothing behind it. There ain't any man that's pulled himself out of a wreck and lived to talk about it that ain't thanked God for bringing him through."

"There's still the men that don't get free of the wrecks. It's an awful way to die."

"Oh, I'd rather I died in my sleep, I ain't going to argue with you on that. But I don't see death the same way you does. I don't see as we're on the losing end. It ain't wonderful getting through maybe, but once we's there I would say we don't remember none of that. It's some kind of life we got then. It's better than anything."

"It would be nice to see things your way. Maybe I could if death weren't so full of pain. But you see what it's like. I believe it's God that's back of it all. I'd say it's him has ahold of death and tells it where to go and what to do."

"Well," Charlie says to me, "I would guess that God ain't got much use for death. You take that cross now. There's your fight between God and death. They went right at her. What come of it, as far as I can see, God made a way of getting us through. You take a look around you and it seems like death come out on top. But no, God has ahold of it, just as you say, and he uses death to get us through. I don't say it's the best of ways. But it's an enemy God's got ahold of and he's working that enemy for the good. I take a look at that cross hanging there and it's a powerful thing, you, a powerful thing."

When I come out of the lighthouse Jonathan Daniel called my name and walked from the woods toward me.

"You been spending time with Charlie Zinck?" he asks me.

"Yes," I says.

"I see him now and again."

"I guess you do. I seen your cross there."

"I got something else I been drawing for him," Jonathan Daniel says, and he pulls a piece of paper out of this notebook he's got in his hand. The picture was of the lighthouse the way you seen it when you was out in a boat at night. The light was shining, but it weren't the usual light. It was like the star he had drawn before. It was so bright and sharp it seemed as if it were burning a hole through the darkness. It gave me that queer feeling again.

"You're coming right along with this stuff, ain't you?" I says. "What are you going to do with all of your drawings?"

"I hate to think of leaving the sea."

"What are you talking about?"

"I'd like to be a priest."

"You mean a minister?"

"No, a priest."

That was all he'd say about it. You could just imagine what Dad would think of one of his boys wanting to become a Catholic. Jonathan Daniel kept it to himself. I don't believe Dad knowed much about the pictures he was drawing either. I think he would of understood them a lot better than he would of understood Jonathan Daniel wanting to be a priest. How I looked at it, all of this was Jonathan Daniel's way of handling him and Joshua almost dying at sea, and Aaron's killing himself. I didn't see it as the best way, but I guess it were better than the way Mom went at it. She looked the thing square in the face and it near drove her mad.

When it come time for the spring trip, Mom had her hair done neat and tight, and she was dressed in her church clothes. She wouldn't hug any of us, not even Dad, but she walked us down to the landing, and didn't she keep up a chatter the whole time. Going on about the weather, and the cooking she was going to do, and how we was to make sure we ate proper on the vessel, and how we was to make it clear to Himmelman that Matthew couldn't have just anybody for his partner. Once we'd launched the dinghy she turned and walked back up to the house. Dad kept a strong face, but I seen he was worried for her. There was an east wind and it took us inside of

Pearl Island and down past Blue Rocks to Lunenburg.

Hank was waiting there on the docks to speak to me. He was still big, still full of stories. We laughed a bit, and then he asks, "You're sixteen now, ain't you?"

"I guess I am," I says.

"You're coming big and strong like your father."

"Yes."

"You still got your father's faith?"

"Hank," I says, and I looks him straight in the face, "I ain't going that way."

"You still got a couple of years to think about it,"he argues. "You don't got to make up your mind today."

"No, Hank. I've made up my mind. I'll stick to the sea."

I seen he was disappointed, so I looked over at Seraphim Levy carrying a couple of huge sacks of potatoes onto the *Heather B Sarty*. Hank's right quiet, but then he puts out his hand and I takes it. He had some strength to him.

"God bless you, Cale," he tells me. "I ain't afraid of what'll come of you. If God's calling you to something, he'll make sure you get ahold of it."

"Fair enough," I says, and I turns and steps aboard the vessel.

Himmelman gives us a speech before the fleet heads out. "You remember how it started out last year," he says, "and you remember how it ended. There wasn't none of you wound up millionaries, but you done all right by that last catch. There ain't no reason we can't have a good trip this time around. You do your work and you mind your own business and the fishing will take care of itself. Besides, we got our lucky piece back this year."

The men laughed and I stood there and smiled at them, but I knowed by then how fast a crew's mood can change. If I went up on deck at night I made sure I always kept my back to the sea. God made no moves. We had a good trip and filled the hold. Matthew fished with Seraphim and he says to us, his head down and one foot working the groove between two planks, "It ain't the same as fishing with Aaron. Nobody's like Aaron. But Seraph ain't so bad."

"All right," Dad tells him, "but you just watch yourself."

"I will," Matthew promises, "but he ain't so bad."

When we come back into Tarragon, Mom looked at us and started crying there in the kitchen. She held Matthew for the longest time and asked him how his new partner was. When his answer satisfied her, she took ahold of each of us and kissed us, she even kissed me, the first time she'd touched me in six months.

"He was a good boy, mother," Dad tells her. "I never heard nothing bad come out of his mouth. And the fishing was fine."

"I'm glad to hear it," Mom says, looking at my face. "I been praying for you, boy."

"Thank you, Mom," I says.

"I wonder what you would think if I asked you to read the Bible to me a couple of hours every day?" she says. "It seems I can't sit still long enough to read. Always got to be getting my hands into something. But was you to read to me, that would be some nice."

"I don't mind doing it, Mom."

"You can start right now then," she says with a small kind of laugh. "I can't say as I've heard any of God's Word read at me since Hank was here last, and that's over a month now. Go ahead, boy. There's a Bible on the table. The rest of you can get about your business."

So I gone back to reading the Bible to Mom just like before, only now she weren't sitting in a chair in the parlour, she were rolling out dough, and making pies, and baking biscuits. I didn't mind it. Anyway I could make peace with her was all right. She'd want me to read to her in the afternoons, so I spent the mornings up at the lighthouse with Charlie. That went much the same. Charlie would talk and I'd listen. Once in awhile I'd argue with him. But he liked that.

One time there was a terrific storm come up, it rattled the walls of the house, freight-train winds Dad called them. We was all of us in the house doing whatever; I was playing checkers with Matthew; Mom was going about the kitchen with her pots and pans as if company was coming. Right through the crying of the wind I heard a sound and I listen, and it's the falling and it's the rising of Charlie's cello. I let Matthew take the game, and then I got up and went to the door.

"Where do you think you're off to in this weather?" Mom wants to know.

"Just a bit of air, Mom," I tells her. "I'll get my coat."

"And your boots."

The wind jumped all over me the moment I'm out the door and the sky a lot of grey muck, like something under your boots, but it weren't raining hard yet, just a spray blowing over everything. By the time I'd made my way up to the light though, the water was hitting on my hands and face like the biting of a swarm of yellowjackets and my cap was flattened and soaked through. I squints up at the lighthouse deck. Charlie was there, this great black bird, all wing and beak, the cello laying across his scrawny legs and the bow in one of his claws. He'd stopped playing and was sitting there in his chair trying to look at the sky tumbling over his head, but all he could do was blink and flinch. He was streaming.

"If I can get you to bring my umbrella up here," he says, "why, I'll take another run at her."

I go inside the lighthouse and this long black umbrella is propped up just inside the door along with a couple of brooms and a ladder. I takes it and I climb them steps to the lantern deck and I step out into that storm. It was some fierce up there, but I got that umbrella open and it was so big it covered the two of us. The only problem was to keep the wind from getting under it and tearing it to pieces.

He went at that cello like he's playing to save his life. It was blowing and the clouds was dirty and crackling with light, but he didn't seem to take notice of any of it. The bow goes scraping across them strings and the notes are coming long and steady and deep. A couple of times it's like he was fitting right in with the snapping of the rain or the grunting of the thunder. After a bit, he starts playing faster, jerking that bow over the strings, the notes short and sharp. It seemed he was after the lightning, his fingers up and down the neck of that cello like a step dancer. He went at it, he went at it, first slow, then fast, notes slashing into your eyes, into your throat, striking down into your gut. I felt like a bar of cold steel and that cello was rasping against me, raising white sparks. Suddenly he gives this short solid stroke with the bow and jumps to his feet.

"Aha!" he shouts, waving that bow over his head.

The wind comes at us, and we head back into the lighthouse and down the steps to where Charlie's got a kettle ready for the woodstove. He makes us some tea and we sit back, I could hardly feel my hands even when I had them wrapped around the mug.

"What was all that?" I asks him.

"Bach's cello suites," he says.

"You had to play them all, did you?"

"Why, boy, I had to play as many as I could. How many chances do you think you get to put man's music up against God's?"

"What did you find out?"

"You heard for yourself. You got to play like wind and sea to keep up with him."

The rest of the day we talked, and when it's dark and I got to head down for supper he puts his hand on my back and says, "Boy, when you come back from the summer trip we'll have our first lesson on the beast."

"I'll be looking forward to that," I tells him as I steps through the door. "Good night, Charlie."

"Good night, Cale. God go with you."

Mom gone down to the landing with us when we're heading out to Lunenburg, and she takes me aside while the others are getting the dinghy ready.

"I wonder if you're still keeping an eye out for your father?" she asks.

"He's doing fine, Mom," I says.

"He can't swim. It don't matter how strong he is, were he to slip and go into the water there's nothing he could do for himself."

"All right, Mom. There ain't nothing going to happen to him. I'm with him day and night. I'll be watching out for him."

"You're good to me, boy," she says, and I gets into the dinghy, and the wind takes us around the east end of the island and out toward Lunenburg Bay.

The fishing was good through June and July. Sundays was full of hymn singing and stories. I was sure something was up, but no, the weather stayed fine, the dress gang had plenty of work, and we never lost a man. It's like God had decided to leave us in peace.

It's a Sunday afternoon we was all up on deck trying to find a bit of shade and there's Seraphim, lying right out where the sun's the strongest. His eyes is near shut, and the sweat's rolling into his beard, and he says, "I'll tell you, a man can take a lot. My Dad was with a couple of others in a dinghy and they was handlining just out of Jeddore. This squall come up, took them right out to sea. They tries to get a bit of sail up to keep her into the waves, but the wind takes that sail and breaks the mast off so they got no more than two or three feet of stump. They gets ahold of their oars then, and what happens but Dad gets one of them pulled out of his hands. They's sure they's going to broach when all of a sudden that wind backs off some. But look, they can't even see the shore, and no way to get back, paddling with one oar don't move that dinghy at all in the swell.

"What do they do? Dad says one of the men told them to lash the oar straight up against the stump and then lash him to the oar. They argues with him, but it's what this man says they got to try. He was about six foot, and by the time they ties his back to the oar and his feet to the stump he's eight or nine feet up. They cuts their second sail into a six foot square and they puts in a couple of slits so they can pass some rope through the canvas and tie it to his arms. Then he grabs ahold of that thing in both of his hands and he spreads out his arms, the breeze tucks into that canvas and bellies her out, and they takes her in for Jeddore. If the wind had of been what it was, it would of tore his arms out of their sockets. But he could just keep a grip on her. It took two hours of sailing to get back and they had to settle for Spry Harbour. Dad says you could hear the insides of the man tearing if it come up a gust. Doesn't know how he kept at it. Says you wouldn't of thought the man had the strength to look at him. Dad was putting water and raw fish to his mouth the whole way back. 'Thank you, Norman,' the man would say to him.

"They gets in and they cuts him down, and he can't move his arms, and he starts bleeding from the mouth. They had to get him to the hospital in Halifax and that almost did him in. But he come out of it. Never got his arms back to what they was though. Dad says they'd always get stiff on him. And when he got a little older, his breathing got bad. He was living up in Port Bickerton and he just died the other year. What do you think of that? What a man can go through if he puts his mind to it. Dad says the man saved them, they would of gone right out to sea and that would of been the end of it."

I guess there wasn't any of us could get Seraphim's story out of our heads. I wondered if the story were true, but a lot of the men believed it. Maybe a week after, Jonathan Daniel takes me up to the bowsprit and it's just coming on night.

"Cale," he says, "I keep having these dreams."

"What dreams?" I asks.

"Almost every night there's this boat going through a storm, and the waves is sweeping her, and the crew is falling off and drowning, and there's this man nailed to the main mast, screaming and twisting his head back and forth."

"Don't tell the other men. They'll get superstitious about it."

"What do you think it means?"

"I don't know. I guess you got Seraph's story in your head."

The fishing had been slacking off, and after moving us around for a week Himmelman says we'll take her down to Sable again if the weather stays fine. The next morning come clear and we hauls up and sails her south and west. Himmelman puts me at the wheel and stands just back of me. The wind weren't so strong, we doesn't get down to Sable till the afternoon of the next day, and all that time I'm hanging onto the wheel, and Himmelman's right there behind me, and not a word out of him. I takes her in and Himmelman drops the anchor at twenty-eight fathom, just off the north-west arm. Then he lets me go down for a nap.

"Two hours," he says, "and I want you up and laying down a couple of sets with your Dad."

Them was burning days. It was coming on to the end of August and the sun and the bits of cloud hung there and never moved. The water's like we was fishing in a pool. And the cod was there. Inside of two weeks we was well on our way to filling the hold. We seen another schooner come in and anchor further up the island. One afternoon Dad and me is waiting on the trawl and two of them comes rowing over from where they's in working close to the shore.

"Looks like Redwis Cross," says Dad. "So that schooner would be the *Sadie Mosher.*"

It was Redwis. Him and his partner come up beside us and Redwis asks, "How's she going?"

Dad moves his chin towards the fish in the bottom of the dory and he answers, "All right."

Redwis looks over at me, his red hair dropping down near his eyes, and he smiles. "I hear you're the good luck of the *Heather B Sarty.*"

"Is that what they're saying?" I asks him.

"That's what Himmelman's telling everyone in Lunenburg."

"I guess he would know."

"I'm glad things is going well for you."

"All right."

"I been turning some things over. I'd like to talk with you again sometime."

"All right."

He looks at me and he's squinting in the light of the sun. "Maybe when we's heading out of Lunenburg next trip?"

"Maybe."

He nods and puts his oars into the water. "I hope you fills your vessel," he says, and they rows back to their marker buoys. We watched them till they was on top of their trawl.

"You're best done with that character," says Dad, and we dips in our oars, and I gets forward to grab ahold of the line and start hauling her in.

The next morning at three o'clock I'm getting up to follow Dad out for some tea, and Jonathan Daniel comes over. He's got that smile of his, the lips hardly turning upward.

"What is it?" I asks him.

"I had the dream again."

I takes a look around, but most of the boys is getting up and making noise.

"What happened?" I asks.

"It were all right," he tells me. "The man on the main mast was all of him bright fire, and the boat all goes to fire, and the sea was fire."

"That's good, is it?"

"Yes. It weren't like ordinary fire. It were God's fire. God comes onto the boat and the boat turns to fire. I got the warm feeling I gets from that drawing. I'd say the dream is a good sign."

"I still wouldn't tell any of the men about it."

"Oh, no," he laughs. "I ain't going to tell no one on this boat, boy. It's just between you and me." And he heads over for breakfast, his long body swaying with the slight motion of the vessel.

What he said to me, it put cold all through me. I went up on deck, but the sky was full of stars and the water was quiet.

"It'll be a fine day," says Dad as we're drifting down to the outside buoy, paying out our trawl. "I would guess we near finish her up today and tomorrow."

"You been praying again, is it?" I asks him.

He laughs. "How do you think we're coming onto all this fish here?"

The whistle blows after a couple of hours and we brings in our fish and heads down for a mug-up. I goes to my bunk to change, my pants was soaked through. A man comes over and sits down across from me on Dad's bunk, and he's holding a cup of coffee.

"I guess that's some good," I says, as I'm peeling off my pants.

"It's a terrible thing to fall into the hands of the living God," he tells me.

I stops and stares at him. No one else is wearing oils that day, but there he is in his, and his face is grim. I didn't know him. You'd of almost thought he was Dad to look at him, but his body was thinner and his hands a lot smaller.

"What are you talking about?" I asks him, but he just keeps looking at me and doesn't say anything more. Then he gets to his feet and goes up on deck.

It's right then I feels something move, not inside of me, but all around me, something was shifting. I pull on my pants and I run on deck, but I'm alone, there's no one up there. And I look out over the water and it's coming on, moving right at me, spreading out over the whole sea.

"Wind!" I shouts. "My God, wind!"

The men come tearing up on deck and the wind, she takes ahold of us and yanks our anchor out of the sea bed and starts dragging us in toward Sable. The air was full of the roar and Himmelman had to scream at the top of his lungs to make himself heard.

"Give me the foresail!" he shouts, and the men run her up, but you can see right off it's too late to tack out of there, we got no room to maneuver.

"Get ahold of the wheel!" Himmelman yells at me. "We got to try and ride her over the arm!"

I grab the wheel and Himmelman puts his hands over mine and helps me steady her.

"Get up the jumbo!" he shouts again, and the boys get her up, and the *Heather B* heels over some and starts running with the wind.

Sable weren't nothing but wave and foam, you couldn't see any of the island and you couldn't tell where the sand started and where it ended. I looked over to the left for the *Sadie Mosher,* but she had already gone onto Sable, you seen her masts sticking out of the water and her hull breaking to pieces in the waves.

"Keep your mind on your business!" snaps Himmelman. "We still got our chance."

We come down to the worst of it and the seas start breaking over the bow some fierce, right away there's five of the dories gets smashed and thrown over the side. We was so close to the sand you seen it sliding over the deck every time a wave broke. All the men was standing in the stern, the bow kept digging into the water, it kept digging into the water. The waves grab ahold of a couple more of the dories and rip them in half, dump all of their gear out over the deck. The hooks and line come swirling around our feet, and Dad says to Himmelman, "We got to get the rest of the dories over the side in one piece."

"All right," says Himmelman.

Dad starts moving toward the bow and at first there's no one goes with him. But then Joshua starts up, hair leaping all over his head like a yellow flame, and he's followed by Jonathan Daniel, beard and eyes black and stiff. Matthew goes forward right quiet, stopping only to pull up his collar with round, white fingers. Seraphim is staring at Matthew's bent body. When two others stagger after Matthew, Seraphim stumbles behind them.

Spray was driving into their faces as hard and white as hail. One man fell and went into the sea, but the others all got there all right. You seen they couldn't stay there long, the bow weren't nothing but water, and the waves kept snagging the bowsprit as if they was going to pull the *Heather B* under head first. Dad and Joshua was going at one dory, and Matthew and Seraphim give them a hand and they pitch it over, but it lands upside down. They got another one and this time they put her over right side up. They's just getting the last one loose and the *Heather B* hit Sable. She come on so fast she split right along her hull and the water come rushing into her and she sinks down.

"Get up!" Himmelman's screaming. "Get up!"

But she couldn't get up. She was filling with sand. She lurches over and the loose dory takes Seraphim and pitches across the deck and through the rail. You could hear Seraphim yelling, and then a whirlpool takes him and the dory right under the hull. And the hull's grinding into the sand.

"Get over the side!" Himmelman shouts at me, and I let the wheel spin through my hands. I start running up toward the bow where Dad and my brothers are crouching, but Himmelman grabs ahold of my arm.

"Jump from here!" he shouts.

"No!" I break free of him and head toward the bow again. The *Heather B* drops down to the right and I fall to all fours, and I'm crawling up the deck. "Dad!" I'm shouting.

I seen him help Matthew jump clear of the vessel. Joshua and Jonathan Daniel had already gone over and Dad was getting ready to make a leap for the dory when he heard me and started back. He grabs me up in his arms and staggers to the side, and he says, "Go, boy, and swim for that dory, for God's sake."

"No," I says, "jump with me," but he takes and throws me as far clear of the vessel as he can. I hit that water and I had a fight on my hands. It was like somebody had ahold of my legs and somebody else had ahold of my arms. I couldn't hardly keep my head up. Then I seen the *Heather B* crack in half and go under, and there's Dad still on deck, he goes right down with her. I starts kicking toward the *Heather B*'s masts, those masts standing clear of the water, but a hand grabs me by the collar and pulls me back.

"Let go of me!" I'm yelling. "I got to get to my father!"

But this person keeps dragging me back so I try to get at him with my hands, I try to twist out of his grip. He gives me a couple of good smacks on the side of the head and that takes the fight right out of me, I pretty well go limp and there's blood in my mouth. He gets me to the dory and he dumps me into it. I take a look and it's Jonathan Daniel.

"You going to stay put, boy?" he asks me.

"The hell with you," I cries. "I'm going back after Dad."

"I'll get Dad. I'm a better swimmer than you are."

"Like hell you are. I'm going back after him."

Jonathan Daniel, he comes up over the side of the dory and hits me full in the face with his fist. He'd got so skinny you wouldn't think he had much strength to him. But that blow laid me out. It was all I could do to lift my head and watch him go, the water burning white.

The
Storm

The Storm

The day of the *Katrina E Zwicker,* it was just as the day of the *Heather B Sarty.* Full of sun, and the water not moving, and you seen this was a lie, but nothing to get ahold of, nothing you could put your finger on. You're rowing in this sun up to the Rock, you're walking on to the lighthouse, you stop to take a look at the water, and it's the same, it's every bit of it the same. And no power in you to keep it from happening, no strength to hold it back.

I gone up and put a chair inside the lantern. The sea was laid out under my feet. You're up and staring down at a world. A couple of boats went out from Blue Rocks, a few more from Lunenburg, and I wrote their names down in my log. The rest of it was the light running over the sea and over the sky, and the blue of it, and you look and it's all falling away from you, falling away to the end of the earth.

God worked it well. Took everyone but me, and there I'm left to walk up from the landing alone. Yes, he had it all set out. Getting us close in to Sable the year before, and me at the wheel, and giving us plenty of fish and good weather to make sure we'd be back. Seeing to it I'm the one brings the vessel in the next year too, and all the men relaxed and thinking I'm God's good luck, and the cod filling the hold, and Dad laughing and thinking it's his praying, and then that wind out of nowhere, and us too close in to Sable, and the vessel going down, all hands, all hands gone.

God knows where I was when I come out of it. There was no shore, no birds, no sun. I made up my mind. Just laid down in the bottom of the dory to die. Wouldn't touch the oars, wouldn't put up the sail. I went on like that for I don't know how many days. Then a fishing vessel out of Shelburne found me.

When I come up to the house on Tarragon, Mom's standing on the porch and she says, "They's all gone, ain't they?"

"Yes, Mom," I answers, and I stops where I am, I don't walk any further. I feel the cloud coming up off the sea and across the island and I feel it over my neck and the back of my hands. Mom was in sun, she was in shadow, she was bright with a brush of cold wind that lifted the edge of her apron and scattered brown hairs across her forehead and throat as if they was strands of grass. She looks over my head at the bay and I feel that too, the water at my back, the ice of it, and for a thousand miles, no face to it, no eye or lip or skin.

"Come here, boy," Mom tells me, and I go on up to her and she puts her arms around me. "The Lord left me one of you."

I'm in bed that night and I hears her crying below me in the kitchen, so I puts on my pants and goes down to her. She's looking at me, and her eyes are small and dark, and her voice is like something scratching in the walls: "I'll kill you for what you done." She gets ahold of the bread knife. I got out of that house and down to Charlie's. She come hammering at the door and she even broke one of the windows, but Charlie locked her out.

"You get him off this island," she's screaming. "I don't want him here. If I gets my hands on him I'll cut his heart out. He's a son of the Devil."

It was Charlie got me off Tarragon and made sure I had enough to get me to Sydney in Cape Breton. He had a cousin was a foreman in one of the coal mines, and when I gave him Charlie's letter he took me on. I wouldn't want to spend my life in them mines, but it was all right for me just then. I was full of anger and I took it out there in the dark.

It's one day after almost two years of this I'm sitting down by the waterfront and I'm watching a couple of schooners take on coal.

Why, they lifts their sails and they ghosts out of the harbour. I could feel the breeze on my hands. I gave the mine my notice the next week and I headed back for the island. It was March, still a bit of winter left to the South Shore. It come a calm day and one of the boys from Chester took me out. I went to see Charlie first, and I told him I wanted to be back near the sea, so I was going to try to make it up with my Mom.

"I'll get my cap," he says, and he puts this godawful brown wreck over his short bristly hair, and the pair of us head up together, him in his shirtsleeves and cap, me in my coat and boots. Mom makes this big fuss over me, and it's decided I'll live with her again and do some inshore fishing to keep the both of us going. She'd had little enough to live on, just a bit of money her brother in Halifax would mail out to her.

I'm back in my old bed and that night I come awake out of a dream, and here Mom's coming into my room. She didn't have no light and I couldn't see what she was up to, so I laid there and didn't say anything. The next thing, she's standing beside me and she sticks this knife deep into my left shoulder. She pulls the knife out, I hear her shoes on the floorboards, she shuts the door, and there's a scuffing on the carpet of the stairs.   As soon as she left the room, I tore my sheet up and tied knots over the wounds. I got dressed, and that weren't so easy, there was blood everywhere and the pain was fierce. I barely got my legs in my pants or did up the buttons on my shirt. I takes my duffle bag and I gets down them stairs hanging onto the wall. I'm out the door and limping over to Charlie's place, and I guess I fell a couple of times. Charlie got me in his bed and gave me a lot of chocolate and coffee heaped with sugar. Then he dressed my wounds as neat as you'd want.

"God's working again," I says to him.

"Don't look like God to me," he answers.

"Oh yes. It's a lot better than having me drown off of Sable."

"Look, boy, never mind God, it's your mother we got to think about getting you away from."

"I ain't going back to the mines."

"I'm not talking about the mines. I'm talking about staying close to the sea. Paul Risser keeps the light over on Bushen's Reef. I was talking with him a few months ago and I see he's made up his mind to retire. If you're interested, I'll speak to him about you taking the light there.''

"Why the hell would I want to do that? I seen God kill enough men.''

"Maybe you could save some.''

What come out of it, I told him I'd drop in on Risser and spend some time with him to see what it was like. Old Risser kept a house in Blue Rocks and I stayed there a couple of weeks. He'd take me out to the light, show me the routine. I can't say what I would of done if that's all there'd been to it. But I seen a vessel come in from the frozen bait trip and nick the reef. This little boy, no more than ten, he's up by the bowsprit and he goes over into the water. A man dove in after the boy but couldn't get ahold of him. The small white body come into Blue Rocks a day later. It's this settled it for me. I told Risser I wanted the job and I headed out to Halifax to talk with my uncle.

Lawrence Goodwin worked for the government and we chatted some. I seen he wanted to give me the job, but he thought I was pretty young at eighteen.

"What makes you think you can handle a light?'' he asks me.

"I been on the sea since I was eleven,'' I tells him. "I went out in the dories at thirteen. A lot of things come at you and you got to handle them. I guess I could keep a light burning.''

He likes that, and he'd got letters from Paul Risser and Charlie, so he decides there won't be any problem me getting the light, he'll put it through. We shakes hands, and I got my cap on and I'm heading out the door, when he says, "My sister wrote me about you being the Jonah of the Fitch household. She got that kind of thinking from our father and she never let go of it. I can imagine how you feel having that over your head. Everyone in our family had me pegged the same way when I was growing up. I didn't want their church and I didn't want their religion. Well, I turned out all right. There's nothing to their talk. It's the Bible that breeds that superstition in them. You stay clear of it all and you won't have any problems.''

So I come to the Rock and its water and winds, I come to the fire between heaven and earth. And I come to the day of the *Katrina E Zwicker*. A sea as wide and quiet as there was, but the black mud of my dreams too, and the soft white corpses under the earth feeding grass and tree and thorn.

I'm staring out past the bay and I see Dad coming back for me the day we gone onto Sable. He gets ahold of me and throws me out into the water and the *Heather B Sarty* goes down under his feet. Matthew turns up his collar with his fat white fingers and glances back. Aaron walks down to the landing with the rifle in one hand and his boots leaving a track in the clean white snow. Joshua stands at the bow of the *Heather B Sarty* and his head is fire. Jonathan Daniel swims away from me into white.

"My God," I says, the words forcing themselves through my lips. "My God, I lost them all."

Joudrey. Shot himself eight years after I pulled him out of the water. Mary. Drowned three years after I got her and her sisters clear of the reef. The crew of the *Christina Covey*. Bought a new boat and went down with her in a storm off of Canso.

"You done nothing here," I whispers to myself, "you saved no one. You can't fight him, he's always had you where he wanted you."

I made up my mind to put out in my dory, row her for all she was worth, take her out to sea. Then I'd let her drift. I'd take no water and no food, I'd lie out in the bottom of the dory. I'd bring the farce to an end. I still had the power to do that with my life.

I gone down the stairs and I'm out the door, and that Margaret Bushen come on the radio. I remember I stood and looked at the sea until she called a third time. Then I turned and went back and says, "It's Fitch here, Missus Bushen."

"There's a breeze come up, Mister Fitch," she tells me. "They got this hurricane south of us and she's changing course, going right up the coast. They was saying they expect her to come onto us by midnight."

"All right, Missus Bushen."

"Mister Fitch. My husband was saying you ought to get in off the reef. It'll be some blow and he seen that reef covered by a southerly. It's what Paul Risser did. Lit the lamp and headed on in."

"All right, Missus Bushen. I'll get on about it."

I went out the door and over to the boat. I got her in the sea, and I'm thinking that instead of heading out I ought to be making my way to the mainland. I'm there with my feet in the water. Living or dying, sometimes it don't make much of a difference to a man. But I seen the flat blue spreading out from the Rock. I seen the sun hanging. I drove a fist into the side of the dory.

"My God," I says. "That's how you're working it. I kills myself or I runs."

I takes the dory and I pushes her out and lets her go. She starts drifting in toward shore and I heads back up to the light. I come inside and I sees the radio and I pulls the dry cells out of her and pitches them out onto the reef. I walks up to the lantern. "By God," I says, "I'll have it out with you," and I lights the lamps right then, the sun still burning in a clear sky, I lights the lamps and sits down in the chair. The flames are going and the lights are turning and I sits there the rest of the afternoon and into the evening, waiting on God.

A couple of hours after, you seen the sky get thick and the sun haze over, it was all hung like with strips of cloth. The boats come running in for harbour and right in after them is the swells, big and heavy and slopping against the sides of the reef. I goes down and gets the woodstove going and I heats up a stew, has it with a lot of dark tea. By six, sea and sky is black. Arms and hands of foam slip over the rocks. "Come on," I says.

The wind's rising and rising till about nine it's thumping the glass of the lantern. I pours some rum into my mug and I stand drinking it, watching the waves jump in out of the dark and grab ahold of the reef. They go at her and they go at her, and pretty soon you can feel the lighthouse shaking, they's getting right in and tearing the rock out from under her. At ten come the snow and it covers the glass so the light can't hardly get out. I throws on my coat and mitts and gets out onto the deck with this piece of wood, scraping the slush off. But you no sooner get her clean and the snow's thick on her again.

The snow was blowing in wet and I stayed out there scraping so the light would come through. I was cold and soaking, and a couple of times the wind got its hands on me and almost pitched me into the rocks. But I weren't about to give up. I kept scratching and scraping and all of a sudden I'm screaming up at him.

That wind started blasting and the snow come to rain and I got pinned up against the side of the light so my head cracked into the glass. Blood coming down my face and I fall there on the deck, pretty near choking on the rain. And by God, the rain was like salt in my mouth. I opens my eyes and I looks out over the rail, and I sees the spray right over the top of the lantern. I tries to get up and the lighthouse gives this lurch and my feet goes out from under me so I almost slide off the deck.

She was blowing. All this roaring, and every sound seemed part of it, but there come a crying, I didn't know what it was. I thought it might of been a porpoise or a whale got dragged into the bay and thrown up on the reef. I'm squinting through the rain and the spray, and all I get is a lot of dark and waves breaking across it like bursts of smoke. Then what looks like this huge mound of rock come through the path of the light and it's a schooner, its spars are tall and black, and there's a man lashed to the crosstrees of the main mast.

I didn't mistake it. He was half-dressed and his hair flat against his head, and when that vessel goes into a wave you seen the whole boat shaking and the masts snapping back, and this man coming up off his lashings like a sail bellying, and he's screaming. Right onto the reef she come, why, her bowsprit broke off against the side of the light. The waves get her and start grinding her into the rocks, and the man's hanging there and his head goes over like he's dead.

I crawls back into the lantern and I pretty well fall down them stairs, my legs and arms are so numb. But the whole bottom floor is water, you can't even see the door, so I climbs to the second floor where oil and spare lumber and a lot of other stuff is stored. I grab up a long coil of rope and a couple of jerrycans of oil. I get the window open there and the waves burst through it, knocking me off my feet. But I time it so's I can dump the oil into the water before another wave breaks. I keep picking up jerrycans of oil, one after another, I must of put ten or twelve into that sea and it was still rough, but right around the lighthouse it smoothed out some.

I tied the rope around my chest, snug up under my armpits, and the other end tight to a beam of wood, and I went through that open window, hit the water, and struck out for the vessel. She was right there, I only gone a hundred feet and the swells lifted me onto her deck. The whole boat was awash, but the masts was still up straight, high above the water. Between the schooner and the light the oil had calmed the seas a bit, but on the windward side the waves was going at the hull, the white of them far over my head. I started up the rope ladder on the main mast, but the wind picked me off and throwed me into the worst of it. I come up for air and I'm being dragged into the middle of the bay. I might of got hauled out to sea, but my rope come tight and I kicked my way back.

I got a wave wrong and near broke my back against the side of the hull, but another throwed me across the deck of the schooner. I fought my way clear of water and oil and got over to the main mast and started climbing the ladder again. I was part of the way up when the boat lurched and the mast pitched over some sharp, it's like I was going at it upside down. The wind started slapping at me from behind and below, I couldn't get away from it.

I kept climbing and I made it to the crosstrees. I grabbed ahold of the man's legs, but he never moved. I had a good bit of my rope to spare so I tied it across his chest and under his arms. I yanked out my knife and cut his legs free. The rope had bit in deep, and his feet was dark and swollen. I reached up and cut his hands away from the wood. The rope had chafed and burned and blood had run down his arms. He fell over my back. The weight was too much, and I seen if I tried to climb back down with him I'd break both of our necks. So I wrapped my hands in the rope of the ladder and hung on and hoped the mast would drop down closer to the sea before the wind tore us loose.

It must of been an hour and the boat starts muttering, you seen the deck split open and the water come through like it's a fountain. The mast went over into the water and the oil and I just got us free of her, she was heading straight down. I seen I couldn't pull us back to the light with only one hand to haul on the rope. So I gathered up the rope between the fellow and myself and I went over on my side, started swimming for the highest part of the Rock. I kept him tight in against the shoulder I had out of the water. I couldn't hardly balance the two of us, and the seas kept breaking over my head, and I'm spitting out oil and saltwater and paddling with my free arm, but if it weren't for the waves going in for the reef I wouldn't of got us there. Most of the Rock was under water, but we fetched up near the bit of hill at the back of it.

That surf's crackling and I hauls us through it on my hands and knees, and all of a sudden we're getting pulled back and nothing I can do about it. I looks and it's the lighthouse is going under. The seas are roaring over the lantern deck and the glass breaks apart and the light goes out. It's busting up and washing away and here I'm tied into it, getting dragged out to deep water. I gets at my knife and I'm hacking away at that rope, took most of my left thumb off, but we come free. I kept ahold of that man and crawled back onto the top of the Rock.

We're maybe six feet above water, and the waves are coming on, so I sat us both up and put my arm around him and hoped to God the seas wouldn't rise any higher. Four or five times a big wave drove into us, but we hung on. It come morning, and everything grey, and there weren't no let up, the rain's tearing across the sky and the sea jagged and the wind at you. At first I'm cold, but after a bit I begins to warm up. The air's white and these huge flames are coming off the tops of the waves. In a few hours it all gone to fire, the sea and the wind and them clouds, they was all bright with it. The roar like some high blaze of driftwood. The air come so hot I put my hands up to it, and I couldn't keep my eyes open, no, it hurt too much. I don't know how long we're talking. I opened my eyes a couple of times and there were strips of fire going every which way, and the sea, when she broke over us, it's flames and you're burning. I didn't care. It was so good to feel something, to feel the heat, to feel some pain going through you.

That afternoon the lighthouse was gone, the storm had slacked off, and they come looking for me in their boats. They found me on that bit of reef that was above water and they brought me in, but they didn't know what to do with me. The only man would take me into his house was Arthur Crouse. I was at Arthur's almost a month, full of fever the first couple of weeks. I remember I seen the stain of my body on the sheets, it was dark yellow, all from the sweat. When I come out of it I had this fever scar on my tongue, you couldn't let nothing touch it. My left thumb was a stump. Made my hand look like a claw.

I was worn out after the fever. Couldn't get out of bed. Just lying there. Arthur comes into my room one morning and shows me this piece of wood with the name *Katrina E Zwicker,* Yarmouth, painted on it.

"The crew must've been washed over the side before she went onto the Rock," he tells me. "Six or seven bodies gone ashore at Cross Island."

"What happened to the man I had with me?" I asks.

"There weren't no man with you?"

"There was a man tied to the crosstrees. I got him down and we sat out the storm on the top of the reef. I had my arm around him the whole time. The sea never took him."

"There weren't no man," Arthur's insisting. "When we come onto you, you had ahold of the mainsail, all rolled up and full of dirt and water. You must of dragged it off of the wreck and swum over to the Rock with it. Nobody knows how you done it, why, it must of weighed a quarter ton. It was covering you and it stopped a lot of the wind, you never got too cold. I would say it kept you alive."

Rose was always in my room when she come back from school. She was near thirteen then, not as pretty as she'd been when she was younger, but this strong face, all serious and determined, eyes that looked straight at you whenever you was saying something she wanted to listen to. One afternoon she says to me, "This was Mary's room, you know."

"Oh," I says. "I didn't think any of you had a room all to yourself."

"She was the oldest."

"Does you miss her?"

"A little."

"Maybe more than a little."

She shrugs and starts moving her finger over the quilt as if she's drawing.

"It don't seem like she's gone," Rose says to me. "I still talks to her now and then. She was good to me. We got to be friends."

"I guess you figure you'll see her again."

"Oh, yes."

"It's nice to have a heaven, ain't it?"

"Yes, but it ain't just that. I think of Aunt Trudy being there and it ain't the same. Mary and me was good friends."

"Maybe you and Aunt Trudy can get that way."

"I don't know. I don't believe we's going to be mad at each other or anything. But I don't think it'll be the same as being with Mary or Dad. I think it matters the way you was with somebody here."

"You ain't afraid to die, is you?"

She stretches her arms up over her head and smiles and tells me, "I would just like to wake up that way."

It's a week later and I'm sitting up in this chair beside the bed, and she comes in. Right off she says to me, "You're leaving soon, ain't you?"

"I suppose I am," I tells her. "You been taking care of me long enough. I got to get out and start looking for a job."

"They's going to rebuild your lighthouse. Dad told me they's going to have it done before Christmas."

I shakes my head. "I'm done with that light."

"Where are you going to go?"

"Home. Back to Tarragon."

"Dad says you don't have no family left. He says you lost them all when you was my age."

"No. I still got my Mom. She's on Tarragon. I'll go and see how she is, look into doing a bit of fishing off of the island."

"When are you going to come back here?"

"I don't know."

"Well, I tell you what, Cale," she says, using my name, and her whole chin shaking, "I'm going to come out to Tarragon and I'm going to marry you."

"Why, what are you talking about? I'm older than your Dad, and by the time you gets to where you wants a husband I'll be like a grandpa to you."

"I'm going to marry you," she says, and her lips is tight and she takes a swipe at one of her eyes. "Dad says none of your family had kids and when you dies that'll be the end of the Fitches on the South Shore. I'm going to marry you and we's going to have a boy."

She takes off out of the room. I never seen her again until the day I was leaving and Arthur was giving me a lift into Chester. She didn't want to come for the ride and she didn't want to give me a kiss. She wouldn't even speak to me. Just stood there by herself on the porch, her eyes dark and her hair dropping over her cheeks and her hands down in her pockets.

It was October of 1957 I come to Tarragon, and that's pretty near thirty year since I left it. I seen a few new houses, the landing was fixed up a fair bit, there were a couple more fish stores. I go up this gravel path. The house stood beside it, fixed up and painted a bright yellow, and there was rose bushes all around it. This thing that'd been nothing more than a piece of skinny wood when I was a kid was right up there, a maple crammed with red and orange. I walked on to Charlie's place, but he weren't home so I gone on up to the lighthouse.

He was supposed to be in his seventies, but his hands was big and full of strength, his eyes sharp as December sea. The only thing, he had a cough. Stones rolling and grinding in a backwash. He puts another chair in the lantern and we sits there looking out over the back of the bay.

"She won't remember you," he says. "She thinks you're dead, thinks you went down with your father and brothers."

She didn't remember me either. She'd lost a good bit of her weight, her hair was white as ice, but she still did it up in a tight bun, and she was still moving around all over the kitchen leaning on this thick cane of black wood. When I told her I was Cale she laughed and said her youngest son had carried that name, so I let it be, told her I was a son of her brother Lawrence and that I'd come to spend the winter, help her out on the place.

"That's good of you," she says. "I can't give you no money."

"I just need a bed to sleep in," I tells her, "and some good food to keep me going. I won't be no trouble."

"Oh," she laughs, "I guess I can still cook a decent meal. My Cale, now he was a good worker and he'd eat a fair bit. You do the kind of work he did and I'll fix you up. You can start with the wood, I ain't got enough for winter. Angus Young's boy Jimmy comes around to do some every now and again, but I ain't seen him for a couple of months."

I got out the axe and went back to the woodpile. I come in with an armful of kindling one morning and she's sitting there with her cup of coffee, and she says, "You know, my Cale was going to be a minister, that's what he had his heart set on. My mother prayed that one of the grandchildren would be a missionary or a minister. But the Lord took him before he was eighteen."

"I'm sorry, Missus Fitch," I says.

"There ain't nothing to be sorry about. It's right the Lord should have his way with things. I don't say I understand half of it. But I guess I shouldn't expect him to explain all of what he's on about to me, should I?"

I'd take Mom on walks around the island, she especially liked going up by the cliffs. She'd lean into her cane there and set and watch the bay spreading out from her.

"Some people hate the sea for what she's done," she says one time. "Three or four of the women out of one of the villages on the mainland left when they lost their husbands off Sable in '26. Didn't want to be near the water anymore. I don't see it that way. My husband always loved the sea. I can imagine what he would of thought of being buried down in the earth. No, he done all right by the sea. She were never cruel to him."

There was a lot of cold that winter and she felt it more than I remembered. She still had that maroon thing, full of threads and hanging on her like a blanket. I bought her another sweater from one of Charlie's nieces who did some knitting and Mom kept that wrapped around her with some of Dad's big old socks on her feet. I had them woodstoves going and she went on about how I got the windows fogged up.

One morning in January she's sleeping in front of the stove in the parlour, and she wakes up with a snort and says, "This would of been Cale's birthday. He'd be, let me see, forty-six, forty-seven, he'd be forty-eight today. Oh, he'd of been some fine preacher by now."

"I guess he would," I says.

"I baked a cake for him one time. Father and me got out the Bible and went through it looking for a good verse to put on it. We finally come up with something, but do you think I can remember it? 'Fear not,' it was. 'Fear not...' No it's gone."

"Fear not," I says, "For I have redeemed thee. I have called thee by name. Thou art mine. When thou passest through the waters, I will be with thee. And through the rivers, they shall not overflow thee. When thou walkest through the fire, thou shalt not be burned, neither shall the flame kindle upon thee."

She looks over at me and she says, "Why, where did you get ahold of that? I believe that's the verse, yes. I didn't think Lawrence would even let a Bible into his house."

"He was good to me. He let me do a lot of things."

"Well, I tell you, my Cale would sit here for hours reading the Bible to me. He never tired of it. I find it hard to read now, my eyes is so poor."

"I'll read the Bible to you if you like, Missus Fitch."

"Oh, no, no. You got a lot of your own work to do around here, don't worry about me."

"I don't mind, Missus Fitch. It's nice to get in from the cold and put up your legs a bit."

That's what we done the rest of the winter. I'd spend the mornings working around the house or getting at the wood, and the afternoons I'd sit in the parlour and read the Bible to her. She'd go off to sleep in an hour, but I'd keep at it and pretty soon she'd be awake again and listening for another few minutes. After supper I'd head down to the store or the boathouse and work at our old gear. Some of it I had to throw away. A lot of it was in fair shape though. The dinghy was gone, but the dories had been under cover the whole time, they was still good. I'd light the lantern and sit there with the trawl over my knees, tying new hooks into the ganges.

The people on the island never said much to me. They was mostly the children of the parents I'd known and they figured I was Mom's nephew like I said. It was only old Missus Young recognized me, and she says once, "God bless you, Cale. Your poor mother was out of her wits when she went after you with that knife. I'm right glad to see you back on the island."

I figured on doing some fishing around the island in the spring, but Charlie sat me down one morning and asked if I didn't want the lighthouse.

"What are you talking about?" I asks him. "It's your work."

"Not much longer it ain't," he says. "I been here a lot more years than I intended. Was I to make sure they'd give you the light, would you take it?"

"I don't like hearing you talk that way. You got a good number of years left in you."

"You's still at arguing with me, ain't you? I told you I don't look at it the same way you does. This body's breaking down on me. I want to go where I can run like a ten year old. I want to think clear. Would you leave your brother's cross up in the lantern?" He coughs and the stones tumble and grate.

"Yes."

"I guess I couldn't get you to pray before you lit the lamp."

"No. I can't forgive God for what he done to my family. I'm

through fighting him. But I ain't about to make him my partner."

"All right, Cale," he says to me. "That's fair." And he pulls his cello out of the corner. "How about the beast? You still want to learn to play her?"

"Yes," I says. "It sort of sets everything out in some kind of order when you plays it."

He looks at me as he's picking up the bow.

"No, Cale," he says, "you don't put any order into the world when you play this thing. The order's already there. How you got to play, you got to go after it, you got to chase it down through the moon and the rain. Then when you finds it, you got to fit into it, you got to keep up with it. And then you'll be playing all right, then you'll be helping to tie things together."

It was January we talked about this and we played that cello every day for the next four months. I come up from breakfast one morning about the middle of May and I seen the light was still burning. Charlie was at the bottom of the stairs, twisted up and cold. I closed his eyes and carried him over to his house.

I buried Charlie and Mom that spring. I'm back from the lighthouse late one night and the house is dark, so I gets upstairs and goes to sleep. Something wakes me and I feel it's Mom standing over me, touching the top of my head with her fingers. She leaves and I fall back to sleep until a choking sound works itself into my dreams and I jump out of bed. Mom's sitting up and coughing blood, it's all over the pillow and the blue of her quilt. I gone to get her a glass of water, and when I get there with it she's lying back and her eyes is white.

"Cale," she says, "it was good of you to come back and take care of me."

I put Mom beside the stone that had Dad and my brothers' names on it, and by God, didn't it have mine? Lost at sea, August, 1926. I put Charlie next to his brothers Ernie and Bill. The same young minister with glasses come and said a few words over each of them, but you seen he didn't know what he was talking about. The family was on the mainland now, they sold Charlie's house to an American woman. She was a writer of some kind and she used it in the summer.

It took getting used to, living in our house all by myself. It's one thing to be on your own in a little light stuck on a reef, it's another to be sitting alone in a big wooden house full of rooms and small noises. I finally closed off most of it, used only the kitchen and my bedroom. As it was, I spent more time down at the store or at the light.

Rose come. We had a small schoolhouse on the island by then and she come to teach at it. Married one of Angus Young's grandsons and settled right in. She was twenty-one when she walked up from the landing with her bags. It was 1964. She got married in under a year. It was at Angus Young's old house and Missus Young was still around to see it. I was fifty-five. I come in the one suit I had. It were clean, but it were too small.

"I guess you need a woman to look after you," says Rose, walking up to me at the reception in her white dress.

"Time's past for that," I says.

"No, I don't think."

She'd come up and see me pretty well every morning before school. By that time they'd put the light over to an electric lamp, this five hundred watt bulb coming off a reflector. You could see it up to twenty miles, I didn't go sitting in the lantern anymore after that. If I weren't fishing, I'd go out on the lantern deck. That's where Rose would find me. She climbs up on the deck one morning and she's in jeans and her hair tied back.

"You sure don't look dressed for school," I tells her.

"We're exploring the island today," she tells me. "It's a kind of nature project. You wouldn't want to join us?"

"No. I guess not."

"Old Mizzly Fitch," she laughs. "What do you do up here all the time?"

"I don't know. I suppose I think some. Easier to do it up here."

"What do you think about?"

"God. He could of gone about things differently. Can't he change anything he wants? But he lets it go. You see it all the time. He lets it run through his hands."

"I always liked listening to you talk. Ever since I was a girl I thought you were special. I thought there was a whole world going on out there on the Rock. You know what I'd like to do? Come by here every afternoon in the summer and talk. Maybe I could even read to you."

"What do you want to spend time with me for? Spend the time with your husband."

"He can't talk to me. He's always going on about boats and fishing and hunting. He drinks."

"He's your husband."

"You don't understand a thing, do you?" Rose snaps. "Why do you think I came out here? To marry Derrick Young? I came out here to marry you. But I knew you'd never do it, all of this about me being too young and you being too old. So I made up my mind to stay here no matter what you did and see to it you had that boy. That's why I married Derrick."

She wouldn't leave off either. She come by every afternoon that summer with her books under her arm. If I'm out fishing, she waits till I come in. She even starts coming over to the house. I don't say it was all her. I didn't try too hard to get her to spend more time with Derrick. I suppose you could say she was a friend. God hadn't given me too many.

She knowed the people was talking about us, but it didn't matter to her. When Derrick found out how much time we was spending together there was a lot of fighting. She'd come over to me full of anger. A couple of times I wouldn't let her go back to her house, you could hear him carrying on, knocking things over and putting his fists into the wall. It was one of them times we started sleeping together.

I remember I felt stiff and dead and cold the first time. She kept asking me what was wrong, but there was nothing I could say. There was another time I sat up in bed and watched her sleep, brown hair over brown skin and small brown fingers curled up in a bar of light. My God, I'm thinking, she's a child, she's young Rose. Then she turned and the way she was sleeping I saw the age in her. A warmth come into me like I'd had whiskey or rum. I kissed her in a clumsy way, the way I'd kissed my aunts when I was a kid. Her fingers reached up to me in her sleep, went along my face and dropped down onto my chest.

Derrick figured out what was going on. One Saturday night I'm there alone and he comes over and blows two windows out of my house with his shotgun. He falls through the door and he's drunk and trying to load two more shells.

"You bastard," he snarls. "I'll kill you for laying your hands on Rose."

But I hit him hard over his heart and that took it out of him. I carried him back to his house and Rose tried to talk to him while I went and throwed the shotgun off of the cliffs. After that night I didn't see much of her. She stayed close to Derrick. I gone on about my business, but I'd think of Rose, her body and her eyes, the strip of sun moving slowly from fingers to arm to face.

She had a baby at the end of April the next year. I hardly seen her in all that time, didn't even know she was pregnant. Derrick was some proud. Even come by the light to ask me over, but I never gone.

It's December and she comes banging at the door, and it was cold, the frost was flashing all over the ground when I opened the door. She come in with the baby wrapped in blankets.

"He's drinking again," she says. "He threw me out of the house."

"You can stay here until he's sobered up," I tells her.

She sits down in the rocker by the kitchen stove and says, "He don't want us back. He thinks the kid's yours. He says you can feed it."

"He'll change his mind."

"I don't think. I told him he was right."

"What are you talking about?"

She unwraps the baby and it's this boy in grey wool, sleeping, his little fists tight. "Looks like you, don't it?" she grins.

"What makes you think it's my baby?" I asks her. "You been sleeping with Derrick."

"Oh, I guess not. I haven't slept with him for two years."

"What are you going to do? You can't stay here."

"Why not?" she says. "You're the baby's father."

"No, Rose. You got to go back."

"I don't. He hits the child, Cale. I come back from school one afternoon and he's drunk and yelling and kicking him around the floor. I'm not going back to him, and if he tries to start something over it he knows what I'll do. Sarah's married a lawyer."

"But you're going to stay here?"

"Well, I'm not going back to Blue Rocks, am I? This is your baby, Cale Fitch, and you got to father him."

That was Rose. More of a schemer than God himself. She had it her way. Derrick gave her the divorce and then he moved off the island. I was watching the ferry rumble away from the new pier and head out around the stone breakwater.

"We drove him to it," I says. "It weren't like it just happened. We gone behind his back."

Rose come and looked out the window. "It was never in my mind to leave him until he started beating the baby. Up till then, all I wanted was to raise a boy for you in Derrick's house. Yes, I was set to bring up a family for Derrick, as long as one of the boys was yours. I had it in my mind to wait until the boy was eighteen and then tell him the truth, get him to change his name to Fitch. I swear that's what I would of done. But when Derrick set on that child I made up my mind to live with you even if you wouldn't marry me."

"It still don't seem right."

"Oh, go on with you. The world isn't perfect. God forgives us. We make our mistakes and we get on with it. You take a look at the Bible and you'll find how many times he brings what he wants out of the bad. How else do you think he could get things done in this world? We aren't exactly a planet of saints, are we? Now, pick up your son, he wants someone to play with. Pick him up, Cale Fitch, and start living out your life."

I tried that. God Almighty, I tried that. Two years we lived together. She lost her teaching job because of it, but that didn't matter to her. All she could see was me and the boy, him growing up, and walking, and spitting out words, and me locked in her brown arms at night. It was the world she wanted.

But I seen another world. I seen my son drowning. I thought of us having a daughter and her choking in her blood in bed. I seen Rose and the life going out of her till she sat in her rocker by the stove and said nothing to anyone again.

I come in from the lighthouse one afternoon and Rose is in the kitchen kneading a mound of dough for bread. There's flour on her apron and on her face. I looks at her and I says quickly, "Rose, you got to leave."

She stops working her dough and stares at me. "What do you mean, Cale?"

"You and the boy. You got to leave. Tomorrow. Next week."

"I don't understand you. Things are fine in this house. We're happy here."

"Christ Almighty, Rose. I know what we are. And I know what's going to come out of it."

"You're not making any sense to me, Cale."

"God. God is at me again. I'm feeling. Feeling for you, feeling for the kid. Things I ain't felt since the *Heather B Sarty* went down. He'll strip me again. Give me heart and then tear it out of me. He'll kill you and the boy to get at me, to break me."

"Cale, this is crazy talk. Sit down."

"It ain't crazy talk. It's what he'll do. I thought he was through with me when he drove the *Katrina E Zwicker* up against the Rock and killed six men I couldn't save. He tore my lighthouse off the reef and left me to die. But no, he ain't finished. He's coming at me till he breaks my soul. And maybe he'll do that. But he ain't taking you and the kid while he's at it. I want you gone."

Rose comes over to me and her hands are stretched out, white to the elbows. "Cale."

I takes her arms and throws her back. God, to see her crying, to see her face breaking down into lines and eyes and strands of hair.

"It's your family," she's groaning, dropping into a chair. "It's their drowning off Sable. It's cut through your whole life. Why can't you see the kid as God's gift to you instead of God's curse?"

"No. I don't forget what God's done. I don't forget what he is. I want you out of the house, Rose. I don't want to know where you go and I don't want to hear from you. I want you and the kid away from me."

I left her in the kitchen, her hands on her face, into her hair, all white. I wanted to swing her up in my arms, get rid of the pain, tell her we'd stick together, see life through. But I had to walk out of the house and head over to the cliffs.

I wouldn't sleep with Rose after that. She figured I was off on this old grief of mine and that I'd come around in a few days. But I stuck to what I'd told her. Her eyes grew larger and darker over the table, across the room, at open doorways. I started spending my nights up at the light.

One evening I come back to get some food from the house and there was only the kid sleeping in his bed. A mug of coffee was on the kitchen table, cold, a spoon stained brown beside it. All her clothes was in the dresser and the bedroom closet. The bed was made, the furniture dusted and clean. I sat down in Dad's chair in the parlour.

None of the neighbours seen her leave by the ferry. No one seen her walking away from the house. A couple of weeks gone by and I was walking along the north side of the island, holding the kid part of the time, letting him run around the rest of it. You never went to that side of Tarragon much, it was all slippery rock and big combers. We come around the side of this huge boulder and I seen some colour. I bent down and it was Rose's apron, folded right neat, a stone keeping it from blowing away.

That evening I took the boy to the light for the first time. The sun was almost gone. We made our way up the narrow staircase that smelled of wood and paint and heat, the kid stumbling and grabbing onto the steps with his hands. He stood in the lantern with the back of his arm over his mouth. I turned on the lamp.

The lantern and our bodies and the glass burst into white and gold as if something had broken open. The kid held out his hands in front of him, opened his mouth as if he was going to drink, gave a cry that was almost a word. He saw Jonathan Daniel's cross and stretched toward it. The fire in the lantern swirled around us, flared off our arms, hurled itself into the night, burned a line across the water.

I carried the kid home. He falls asleep against my chest. I let him stay there. I never slept, just sat with him breathing into my shirt and chest, Dad's chair creaking whenever I shifted my weight, the house as bright and as dark as the sea.

GLOSSARY

bait tub	wooden bucket in which baited trawl line is coiled and placed in the dory
cable	anchor line
Cortland	a variety of apple grown in the Annapolis Valley of Nova Scotia
dress gang	those specifically designated to dress down or clean the catch
dulse	curly black seaweed
fish store	a shed in which small quantities of cleaned fish are stored as well as various types of fishing gear
flunky/catchy	that individual of the dress gang who removes the tongues and cheeks of the fish
ganges	short ropes with hooks that are attached to the main trawl line
groaner	buoy used to mark hazardous areas often fogged in and which makes a groaning sound as it is rocked by ocean swells
header	that individual of the dress gang who removes the heads of fish

high liner	one who catches a large quantity of fish
kipper	a smoked fish with a dark reddish colour
lantern	that top part of a lighthouse which houses the lamp
lantern deck	that railed and sloping outside deck which surrounds the lantern
light	lighthouse
point blanket	a type of heavy woollen blanket
quintal	a form of weight measurement (112 pounds)
slop ice	a slush ice that forms on the ocean's surface when the day is windless and cold and the ocean is very calm
throater	that individual of the dress gang who slits fish open and removes their entrails
thwarts	the seats across a dory or small boat
trawl	one long continuous line to which are attached hundreds of baited hooks
wrackers	those who strip a shipwrecked vessel

Afterword

I can think of no better introduction to Murray Pura's *Mizzly Fitch* than Ralph Wood's essay, "In Defense of Disbelief." He concludes this compelling and incisive piece with a reference to a character from the fiction of Peter De Vries:

> Don Wanderhope refuses to believe that his daughter's death is either the mechanical execution of a divine plan or the random result of godless chance. His encounter with . . . Christ suggests, instead, that God has strangely subjected himself to the sin and rage of his people. This is indeed a dark revelation. . . . Yet his fiction makes powerful witness against the soggy spirituality of our age, confronting us with a Cross which demands our disbelief in all sentimental substitutes. (*First Things*, October '98)

Pura confronts us with a similarly dark vision, developed through the tormented consciousness of Cale Fitch, a lighthouse keeper, whose pathological preoccupation with the problem of evil has twisted and determined his life. Haunted by the apparently cruel and senseless deaths that frequently claimed the fishermen of his South Shore island community during the early decades of this century, and justifiably dissatisfied by the naïve and ill-conceived attempts of his parents and pastor to account for these deaths, Fitch employs his beacon and brawn to wage war with God, dedicating himself to redeeming a few lives from a deity who, to this profoundly disturbed spirit, appears no better than a predatory shark. Although many of the believers within his community (and indeed many of his readers) may see him as simply blasphemous, he is arguably the most rigorously religious character in the book, and certainly the one most radically committed to the integrity of the faith as he has received it. Unlike those who too easily fuse pagan superstitions with Christian theology or simply refuse to pursue the implications of God's sovereignty within a world riddled by tragedy, Fitch insists on answers, and revolts violently when he believes he is denied them. Yet his habitual refusal of false comfort unquestionably blinds him to the hints of genuine resolution and rest that lie beyond the narrow terms of his obsession. For as in De Vries' fiction, this novel clearly gestures towards a terrible good, towards a burning, crucified figure, who truly meets us on the raging waters, pierces our darkness and guides us home.

Given that Pura was born and raised in Winnipeg and is of Ukrainian descent, one might not have anticipated that his first novel would centre on the lives of Nova Scotia's South Shore fishermen, let alone tackle the theological tensions such a life may generate for these typically conservative, Protestant communities. But though a stranger by birth to this world, he became one of its intimates through marriage and vocation. Linda, his wife, comes from a South Shore family, her father being a commercial fisherman from a family of fishermen. Pura himself lived on the South Shore for two-and-a-half years, and also pastored a church there for part of this time. Although he has since moved to Western Canada, he and his family return regularly. And what he could not learn from his immediate contacts, he learned through research, for his formal education—including a Master's of Divinity from Acadia University and Master's of Theology from Regent College—testifies to both his abiding passion for history and his keen historical sense. His accurate ear for what one Maritime reviewer called the South Shore "patois" may be attributed to his training in theatre, another abiding passion. And though his decision to employ this dialect in an intimate first-person narration may seem nervy for an outsider, he carries it off rather well, as this same reviewer (perhaps grudgingly) admits.

I taught *Mizzly Fitch* for several years, in part because it explores the theme of entrapment around which I organized my Canadian Literature course, entrapment arising especially from conflict between exceptional individuals and their social environment. The novel proved very successful, no small achievement given the company it kept, which included works from Atwood, Lawrence, Munro and Vanderhaeghe. Indeed, one student who studied the work in her freshman year with me, and who has now just completed a Master's degree in English, recently confessed that this novel had the biggest impact on her of any work she studied to date, again no small accolade.

Perhaps some of this impact arose from the presence of the author himself, because whenever possible, I arranged for Pura to read for the class and then answer questions. Some questions touched on the more seemingly fantastic elements in the plot, such as the mystical experiences of the brothers at sea prior to their rescue, which Pura assured the class, were loosely based on historical accounts. And other questions concerned the vocation of writing itself, the trials of publishing, and so on. Invariably, however, the questions veered around to touch (and then linger) on the possibly autobiographical elements in the work. That Pura was (and is still) a pastor, and yet wrote such a darkly probing work, fascinated them, and many clearly wanted to explore their inklings that there was something of Cale Fitch in him, and that he must surely have suffered personal tragedy to write with such a sense of anguish and anger. He denied any direct autobiography, however, pointing out that Fitch's crisis lay dormant within the community itself, which had suffered horrific loss—as the numerous gravestones in South Shore cemeteries attest—and yet affirmed faith in a benevolent, omnipotent deity. In a sense, it only required a particular consciousness to bring it to acute focus, and Pura simply provided that consciousness in Fitch. As true as this may be, Fitch's revolt does take a highly idiosyncratic form, which is both consistently and perceptively developed, suggesting at very least the author's strong imaginative sympathies with his character.

Although the response to the novel was decidedly enthusiastic, some aspects of the work troubled the students, notably the structure, which they found slightly confusing and the ending, which they found slightly compressed. And I must reluctantly confess that I share some of these sentiments. The three part- structure—"The Light," "The Sea," and "The Storm"—partitions the text into sections that do not correspond to some of the key developments in Fitch's life or to the temporal orientation of the narration, and readers need to be aware of this to keep things straight.

"The Light" opens with the words, "No. I don't mind telling the story. I am Mizzly Fitch. And them two vessels, the *Heather B. Sarty* and the *Katrina E. Zwicker*, them and that lighthouse, why they's the spindle and wheel and foot that run my life out. . . ." This introduction suggests that these two events will frame the tale. But this is not the case, for he has not yet met Rose (as adult rather than child) at this point, as is evident from certain of his comments about the nature of his relationships to date. And their relationship remains one of the most significant—if enigmatic—aspects of the narrative. Another possible confusion arises from the suggestion at the conclusion of the first section that Fitch is narrating the next section to Arthur Crouse, whom he has just rescued from the sea. But this proves a superfluous contrivance, for nowhere do we have a sense of this specific audience, and it seems to serve no thematic or dramatic purpose.

The middle section, "The Sea," the largest in the book, straightforwardly traces the development of Fitch's obsession, from his childhood to the wreck of the *Heather B. Sarty*. The final section, "The Storm," jumps ahead many years to the day of the second shipwreck, the *Katrina E. Zwicker*, thereby taking us back roughly to where he begins the first section. Yet mid-way through the final section, the story moves beyond the temporal framework and temporal perspective established by the opening section, thereby departing from both the subject matter and retrospective narration of the earlier sections, and perhaps confusing readers.

As intimated, the latter half of the short final section also introduces, complicates and "resolves" his crucial relationship with Rose. Such compression of time towards the end of a novel is not necessarily a flaw, though in this case one cannot help but feel that Pura needed to explore the genuinely disturbing nature of this relationship and its outcome in more depth. Similarly, one might also wish that Charlie Zinck, whose perspective on the problem of evil Pura clearly privileges, had appeared in the text earlier and attracted more attention. But these are minor limitations within a work abounding in strengths, and, ironically, also testify to Pura's capacity to make us care deeply about this narrative and these characters.

Other readers may have trouble with *Mizzly Fitch* for thematic rather than technical reasons. While the work has a certain charm as a period piece with distinct local colour, the novel proves essentially theological, and narrowly so, in that it explores the consciousness of a character consumed by the problem of evil. Two loosely-defined classes of readers may thus find themselves at odds with the work: those who identify quite closely with the conservative religious culture against which Cale revolts, and those secular (or theologically-liberal) readers for whom Fitch's struggles are virtually meaningless. To begin with the latter, the problem of evil in its strictly theological form only arises within a context where people affirm that evil exists within a world governed by a benevolent, omnipotent deity. Denying one (or more) of these conditions dissolves the heart of Fitch's problem, and makes him at best a pathetic, if somewhat interesting, anachronism. Readers in the former class are likely to have more severe problems, in that the novel may simply offend them—even though such offense, as I hope later to show, is ultimately unjustified. The risk of offense arises from a number of sources: a sense that Pura has distorted the culture, producing a caricature for his own polemical purposes; a sense of *lèse-majesté* in the face of Fitch's blasphemy; and perhaps even, a sense that Pura is probing the reader's own darkest, secret, fears.

Some of the possibility of offense evaporates once we make the necessary distinction between Fitch's perspective on the problem of evil and the novel's (not to mention Pura's). For while the novel develops the problem of evil within a broad biblical tradition, such as that established by the book of Job, which it cites directly, Fitch's particular troubles fall more closely within the thematic concerns of the book of Jonah, which also finds repeated mention. In other words, the novel suggests that Fitch's development is driven as much by his Jonah-like refusal to see solutions as it is by his capacity to see the problems in the first place, that this lighthouse keeper, as it were, keeps the light focused on others because he fears to have it focused on himself.

The problem of evil also takes a very explicit and slightly unusual form in Fitch's mind, telling us as much about the man as it does the world in which he lives. It develops in the boy from the close conjunction of two events: the accidental death of his uncle Tremaine, and the reading of a book about the capricious and cruel antics of Greco-Roman deities. That his parents (particularly his mother) deal ineptly and insensitively with the traumatized child no doubt also exacerbates the crisis. Receiving no satisfactory answer, Fitch deconstructs and then sinisterly reconstructs the central narrative by which his culture lives. And in this new—and still thoroughly religious—narrative, Fitch features as the protagonist and God (the death dealer) as the antagonist, or rather Fitch as crippled God and God as omnipotent devil. In either case, for all its courage and heroic appeal, it is a decidedly monomaniacal vision.

It is also important to note that there appears to be some philosophical confusion in Fitch's mind. Generally, those who formulate the problem of evil include suffering of all kinds, but Fitch fixates on death alone, even identifying God with death at one point. When someone points out the inevitability of death, however, he switches tacks, and argues that Tremaine—indeed all those who die at sea—need not die suffering and (by implication) in terror. Yet suffering of all kinds appears woven into the essential fabric of this community that wrestles its living from the harsh and dangerous seas, and, given his position on his uncle's death, it is surprising that this general suffering attracts his attention not at all. And the fear of which he complains seems peculiarly Fitch's own, and perhaps derives more from the prospect of losing control than from the prospect of suffering itself. Such a fear, uniquely acute in Fitch from the beginning, would help explain the severity of his response to untimely death. This is not to say that the book does not examine the problem of evil in its broader, more traditional forms, for Pura accosts us with graphic accounts of the horrors of trench warfare, as well as with appalling domestic tragedies. Fitch's consciousness, however, determines the shape of the dominant problem, and this problem proves uniquely his own.

The novel offers a number of possible solutions to the general problem of evil, some of which obviously hold more promise than others. When his parents and pastor attempt to attribute his uncle's death to accident or the devil, Fitch vigorously objects, arguing for a rigorous understanding of God's sovereignty. Much less convincing (and less excusable) is his father's reference to the sea "coming for payment." There is simply no place for this incipient polytheism in Christian theodicy, and Fitch again rightly rejects this, as he consistently does all forms of superstitious paganism. Other characters deny the reality of the problem itself, either by espousing atheism or Deism, but neither position carries any conviction for Fitch. More hopeful is his father's appeal to the so-called Free Will Defense to account for personal tragedies that people either directly cause or willingly make possible. But this defense cannot account for "natural" disaster, so it cannot satisfy.

That the novel successfully points to the possibility of genuine satisfaction identifies its accomplishment and perhaps Pura's true strengths as a writer, for he is more poet than philosopher, more passionate mystic than systematic theologian, and works more effectively through images than explication. Indeed, he mediates his central theological insights though images, and we must attend carefully to these if we are to discover the coherence and comfort at the heart of this work. Two characters figure largely here: Jonathan Daniel (Fitch's brother) and Charlie Zinck, one a prophetic visual artist and one a mystical musician. (As an aside, it is interesting to note that William Pura, the author's brother, is both an accomplished visual artist and composer.) Jonathan Daniel's insights develop significantly over the course of the novel, beginning with a vision of God as a dangerous, impersonal, Heraclitean fire that runs through all nature, and maturing into a recognition that this salvitic fire breaks down and consumes everything in us that keeps us from intimate relationship with our creator and source. Fitch typically shudders at Jonathan's vision, at both the scorching drawings and oracular pronouncements, not so much because of the physical suffering that he knows must be involved in such a process, but rather because he refuses to suffer the knowledge of himself that would accompany exposure by the relentless light. Charlie's music and insights are more explicitly Christian, and more directly connected to the problem of death. One should note, however, that Charlie's description of our post-resurrection experience assumes the unity to which Jonathan Daniel's sketches testify. Conversely, Jonathan Daniel eventually discovers what Charlie argues all along, namely that we need not fear death, for we die neither pointlessly nor alone. As Charlie insists to Fitch, "I never knowed [Christ] but to die with every one of them."

In a sense, Fitch—or at least a significant part of Fitch—dies with the wreck of the *Katrina E. Zwicker*. Certainly, it changed him profoundly, as Fitch himself admits, and everything that happens after this should prove both dramatically and thematically unimportant, which again locates one of the difficulties with the subsequent Rose episode. The wreck, however, truly is the climax of the novel, and shows Pura at his best. The whole incident is wonderfully rife with irony, a fitting climax to the life of this man who wields the light in order to hide from it, saves others from death in order to quell his own morbid fear, and who does God's work in order to frustrate God. Thus it is particularly fitting that on the day of his ultimate despair, and in defiance, he should "save" God and thus be saved himself. And though Fitch does not recognize the man lashed to the crosstrees, we know him to be the heart of Jonathan Daniel's visions and Charlie's music, the consuming fire, the bright conqueror of death who sticks closer than a brother. Through this act, at once defiant and faithful, Fitch proves his parents prophetic when they gave him his life verses, and that beyond any possibility of human understanding or engineering. Here and here alone, in a will and compassion beyond either our desires or imagination, we may find true shelter from the storm, true rest for our souls:

Fear not, for I have redeemed thee. I have called thee by name. Thou art mine. When thou passest through the waters, I will be with thee. And through the rivers, they shall not overflow thee. When though walkest through the fire, thou shalt not be burned, neither shall the flame kindle upon thee.

—Stephen M. Dunning
"Bobbie Burns Day," 1999